To Be Continued . . . .

volume two

. . . . Gordon j. h. Leenders

ECW Press

FIC Leend

Leenders, G.
To be continued--. Volume
two.

PRICE: $19.95 (3559/cl   )

Copyright © Gordon Leenders, 2006

Published by ECW PRESS
2120 Queen Street East, Suite 200, Toronto, Ontario, Canada M4E 1E2

All rights reserved. No part of this publication may be reproduced, stored in a
retrieval system, or transmitted in any form by any process — electronic, mechanical,
photocopying, recording, or otherwise — without the prior written permission
of the copyright owners and ECW PRESS.

LIBRARY AND ARCHIVES CANADA CATALOGUING IN PUBLICATION

Leenders, Gordon j.h.
To be continued . . . volume two / Gordon j.h. Leenders

ISBN 1-55022-668-1 (V.1)
ISBN 1-55022-720-3 (V.2)

1. Title

PS8573.E359T6 2005   c813'.6   C2004–907048–7

Editor: Jennifer Hale
Cover and Text Design: Tania Craan
Cover Image: ©Damir Frkovic/Masterfile
Typesetting: Mary Bowness
Printing: Transcontinental

This book is set in AGaramond

The publication of *To Be Continued . . . volume two* has been generously supported
by the Canada Council, the Ontario Arts Council, and the Government
of Canada through the Book Publishing Industry
Development Program.

Canadä   Canada Council for the Arts   Conseil des Arts du Canada

DISTRIBUTION
CANADA: Jaguar Book Group, 100 Armstrong Ave., Georgetown, ON L7G 5S4

PRINTED AND BOUND IN CANADA

ECW PRESS
ecwpress.com

To my mothers:
Henny and Brenda
&
my sisters:
Yvonne and Sharon-Anne

so, what's next?

"Montreal . . . I know. I'm *so* excited . . . No. I've never been. Have you? . . . And? . . . That's what people keep telling me. Everyone I talk to says they absolutely adore Montreal at this time of year . . . Hmmm? . . . Are you kidding? I've had my suitcase packed for two weeks already. It's all I've been thinking about . . . Of course I will. I'll call as soon as I get back and let you know how things went . . . Thanks. I'm sure I'll have a great time. And thanks so much for calling, Marie. *Au revoir!*"

Smiling as she hung up the phone, Eileen reluctantly returned her gaze to the haphazard collection of clothes she'd pulled out of her closet and thrown on the bed moments before Marie had called. Sundresses, skirts, and shorts lay intertwined with wool sweaters, long pants, and jackets. Her smile faded as Eileen sighed and shook her head. She had no idea what to pack. She'd stopped checking the weather reports for Montreal last Thursday, the day her husband, George, told her he wasn't going with her. "For all I know it could be raining all week," she muttered to herself, shoving aside the still empty suitcase lying on the floor beside the bed. "Or hot and humid. Or unseasonably cool. Or . . . oh, why am I even bothering? I should just call and cancel the whole —"

"You're still going?"

The sound of George's voice caused Eileen to jump. What's *he* doing here, she wondered, not turning around. He wasn't due back from his shift for hours. In fact, the last thing he said before leaving this morning was, "I'll see you after work," as though he expected her to be home when he returned, no doubt thinking that because he'd said he wasn't going on the trip, neither would she.

Then it hit her: maybe he's changed his mind and decided to come with me! A rush of excitement and expectation swept through Eileen. Barely able to resist the urge to squeal with delight, she spun around and saw her son, Cody, standing in the doorway to the bedroom.

The smile on Eileen's face dissolved immediately. She should've known better. Cody sounded so much like his father nowadays. Well, at least how his father used to sound.

"Of course I'm still going," Eileen said, doing her best to hide her disappointment.

"Without Dad?"

Eileen shrugged. "That's *his* decision, not mine."

"But I thought the trip was supposed to be for you *and* Dad?"

"It was."

"Well, what about Dad?"

Turning back to face the pile of clothes on the bed, Eileen scooped up a sweater, looked at it for a few moments, then shook her head and set it aside. "Your sister told me once that the definition of insanity is doing the same thing over and over and expecting a different result each time."

"What's that supposed to mean?"

"Well, for starters, it means I'm through thinking your father is ever going to change," Eileen said, snatching the floral-patterned sundress George bought her last spring off the bed and flinging it in the direction of the closet. "It also means I'm through trying to get him to change. And, it probably means —"

Eileen hesitated, not knowing whether she should complete her thought. She stared at the sundress now laying in a crumpled heap on the floor in front of the closet. "It probably means our marriage is through."

"What? Mom, you're joking, right?" Cody said, taking a step into the bedroom.

Eileen shook her head. "Not this time, I'm afraid."

"Why? I mean, what happened?"

It was the concern in her son's voice that made Eileen pause and reconsider her tone. "Oh, I don't know, really," she said, softly, continuing to sort through the clothes. "It's a long story. Too long. And far too complicated. I wouldn't even know where to begin."

Cody moved further into the bedroom, loitering momentarily at the foot of the bed before taking a seat on the edge of the mattress, filling the spot left vacant by the discarded sundress. "I thought you and Dad got along great," he said, his voice trembling with emotion. "I mean, everyone's always talking about how the two of you met. They're always going on like it was the most romantic thing they've ever . . ."

In the moment before Cody's voice trailed off, Eileen saw tears forming in his eyes. "Oh, Cody," she said, shoving aside some clothes before sitting down next to him and taking his hand. "I'm not saying our entire marriage was bad. Your father and I had some great years. Magical years. We used to say we weren't happily married, we were *blissfully* married. And we were. But things changed. We had you and Cailey and then —"

"Wait a second," Cody said, abruptly pulling his hand away from Eileen's. "Are you saying the reason you and Dad might get a divorce is because of me and Cailey?"

"Oh, honey, of course not. Your father and I knew things were going to change. We realised that once we had children we wouldn't be able to do the things we used to do — and we were fine with that. But we also promised each other that as soon as you and your sister were out of the house, we'd try to get our old lives back."

"Oh," Cody said, putting his hand on the bed. "And so you're angry that you haven't?"

Eileen nodded, once again taking hold of Cody's hand. "And disappointed. And tired. Tired of trying for the both of us. I thought winning this trip might have changed things for your father. It seemed to. At least for a little while. But then he went back to his old routine.

Back to just going to work, then coming home and watching sports and sitcoms all night."

"But that's just Dad. He's always done that."

"Not always, honey. Before you and Cailey were born, he never watched TV. Never. He did other things. *We* did other things. We used to —"

"I know, I know. You guys used to go for hikes all over the city."

"No," Eileen said, shaking her head. "I'm not talking about just that." Then, after a few moments' deliberation, she threw up her arms and said, "For God's sake, your father and I haven't made love in over six months."

"Mom!" Cody shouted, covering his ears with his hands. "That's way too much information. *Way* too much."

Eileen laughed, surprised — by both her admission to Cody and the uncomfortable reality of her statement. Six months, she repeated to herself. Had it really been that long?

"I can't believe you just told me that, Mom."

Eileen shrugged. "Well, it's true."

"Yeah, okay. But I still didn't need to know it," he said, now smiling at her through his scrunched-up face.

Eileen reached over and hugged him. It was good to see him smiling again. He looks so much like his father, she thought. So much like the man I fell in love with.

"So," Cody said, his voice once again taking on a more serious tone. "Do you really think you and Dad will get divorced?"

Letting go of Cody, Eileen nodded her head slowly, thoughtfully. "I'm just beyond the point of caring right now, honey. And, as far as I'm concerned, I think it's best if your father and I go our separate —"

Oh, Eileen, you're such a fool, she thought to herself, sniffling and subtly daubing the corners of her eyes with a napkin.

It was probably the tenth time Eileen had replayed the conversation she'd had with her son before departing for Montreal two days ago. She had to admit, she'd certainly put on a fine show of strength

4

(or was it stupidity?) for Cody. But now, less than forty-eight hours later, seated alone in a café hundreds of kilometres away from the sanctuary of her own home, she was having second thoughts about the sincerity of her statements.

What was I thinking? she wondered, pulling a pair of sunglasses from her purse and putting them on in an effort to hide her tears. Oh, Eileen, you really are a damn —

"*Excusez-moi*, Madame. Is this your first visit to Montreal?"

For an hour and a half, Eileen had been seated on a patio, sipping tea and quietly observing early afternoon drift into mid-afternoon along Rue Saint-Denis, her thoughts occasionally distracted by the ever-changing street scene: the steady stream of upscale shoppers attached to swanky purses and designer tote bags sharing the sidewalk with the young and the homeless; the whoosh of cars sprinting from traffic light to traffic light every thirty seconds; and the occasional murmur of a foreign language temporarily eclipsing the melodious mixture of French and English accenting the warm summer air.

This was Eileen's second afternoon in Montreal. She'd spent the first afternoon settling into a private suite in a charming little bed and breakfast overlooking Parc Fontaine. After unpacking and getting better acquainted with her hostess — who thankfully spoke near perfect English — she'd had a short nap before freshening up, changing into casual clothes and going for an early evening stroll in the park. An hour later, after watching a free concert put on by a steel drum quartet from Martinique, she was seated on the lawn near Lover's Lake, rereading one of her favourite Danielle Steel novels while nibbling on the cinnamon bun she'd purchased in Union Station prior to boarding the Via train.

Shortly before 9:30 PM, when it became too dark for her to continue reading, she'd spent some time admiring the seemingly endless parade of people passing through the park until the sight of a middle-aged couple holding hands, laughing, and embracing each other, prompted Eileen to abruptly abandon her position. Stifling her tears, she hastily wrapped the remainder of the cinnamon bun in a napkin, placing it and the novel in her purse, and then walked quickly back to her B&B, collapsing on the king-sized bed and crying herself to sleep.

This morning she awoke early, had a shower, dressed quickly, read two more chapters of her novel, and was about to start a third when she heard a woman speaking to the B&B hostess in the kitchen downstairs and decided to see who her fellow guest was.

Despite still having almost no appetite, Eileen forced herself to eat a bowl of fresh fruit while chatting amicably with the woman, a divorcée from Pennsylvania with a tart sense of humour who admitted to being much happier without her husband, likening him to a bad case of indigestion. "I'll tell you how I spelled relief," she'd said, laughing. "D-I-V-O-R-C-E!"

Determined not to spend another day feeling sorry for herself, Eileen accepted the woman's invitation to visit some local attractions. After a tour of the Biodome, they'd had a coffee at a nearby eatery before taking a taxi back to the B&B.

Eileen had hoped to continue spending the afternoon with her new friend, but, unfortunately, the woman had another engagement. Eileen instead decided to stroll along Rue Saint-Denis, hoping that some window-shopping, reading material, and the busy street would distract her enough to avoid another episode of tears.

In an effort to appear more *bon chic*, Eileen had changed into a sleeveless silk blouse, a gypsy skirt, and her new leather sandalettes, brought along a pair of what she thought were stylish sunglasses, and swapped her Danielle Steel novel for a French fashion magazine. After window-shopping for almost an hour, she'd located an empty table on a street-side patio and sat sipping tea, flipping through her magazine, and enjoying her anonymity until the man seated at the table beside her said something that caused Eileen to stop thinking of her conversation with Cody and wonder why on earth someone would think this was her first visit to Montreal.

Initially, Eileen thought — hoped, actually — that the man was speaking to someone else, perhaps the young touristy-looking blonde with the knapsack seated at the table in front of Eileen, but then, sensing his eyes on her, she stole a quick glance in his direction and saw that he was gazing inquisitively at her.

"I am sorry," the man was now saying, in slightly accented English. "I did not mean to interrupt you. I merely ask you if this is your first visit to Montreal?"

Wearing dress pants, a white linen shirt, dark sunglasses, and no wedding ring, Eileen put the man's age at fifty, give or take a couple of years.

"Oh. Why . . . yes. It is," Eileen replied, softly, not wanting her confession to reach the café's other patrons, wondering how the man was able to so easily detect her ruse. "Does it show?"

When the man pointed to the English version of the Montreal guidebook poking out of Eileen's purse, she shoved the book out of sight, smiled, and said, "I guess it does."

The man returned her smile, then made a gesture to reassure Eileen that her being a tourist was perfectly acceptable, before asking permission to join her.

Ten minutes after removing their sunglasses and exchanging formal introductions (his name was Jacques Donnet), occupations (he was the owner and executive chef of a thriving bistro in New Orleans), and reasons for being in Montreal (he, too, was on vacation), they had fallen into easy conversation.

"So, you are not with your husband then?"

"Oh. Yes. Yes, I am. I mean, not at this very moment, no, but we are most certainly together," Eileen stammered, nervously twirling her wedding ring while telling herself to relax. "I'm sorry, Jacques," she said a few moments later, taking a deep breath and letting it out slowly in an effort to compose herself before proceeding, "what I meant to say was, my husband and I are neither divorced nor separated. He is just not with me on this vacation."

"I see," Jacques said, smiling at Eileen's clumsy response. "And, this is normal for you, yes?"

Eileen hesitated, considering the question for a moment. Some-where between saying the word 'divorced' and admitting George was not with her, she'd felt her stomach tensing, her nose prickling, and her eyes beginning to water. She wished she hadn't taken off her sunglasses.

"The trip was supposed to be for us," Eileen replied, her face tinged with sadness. "We won it. Last summer. Actually my husband won it. And now, here I am, alone in Montreal."

Jacques nodded his head, slowly, as though he was mulling over what Eileen had said. "I suppose there are much worse places to be alone, *non?*"

Eileen nodded. "I know. It's just that we've always done things together," she replied, reaching for her sunglasses and putting them on again. "We've never been apart for this long before. Ever."

Jacques gently massaged his clean-shaven chin. "I understand it is important to hang on, yes. But it is also important to let go, *non?*"

Eileen sighed. "I guess." A tear slid out from under the bottom rim of her sunglasses, making it halfway down her cheek before she hastily wiped it away. "I'm sorry."

"There is no need to apologise," Jacques replied, reaching inside his pant pocket and pulling out a freshly folded handkerchief, handing it to Eileen.

"Thank you," Eileen said, gently patting her cheek with the hand-kerchief.

"In fact," Jacques said, leaning forward, his voice gentle. "It is I who should apologise. I make it sound easy. But I know it is very diffi-cult to let go."

"Are you divorced?"

Jacques shook his head. "Married. To the most demanding woman I have ever met. My bistro."

Eileen laughed.

"It is no joke. She is a slave driver, that woman. I work and work and work — and still she wants me to work more. Always I am on my toes, making sure everything is just so for her. But, two years ago, I put my feet down. I tell her, 'That is it. I have had enough. I must relax. I must let go. Even if it is just for a few days.' *Et voilà*, it works. I am a new Jacques when I get back to her. Maybe you and your husband are the same. Maybe you need to let go for a while?"

Eileen smiled. "Maybe," she said, removing her sunglasses and daubing her still-soaked eyes with the handkerchief before handing it back to him.

She wondered what George was doing right now. She glanced at her watch: 3:34 PM. He's probably in front of the TV, she said to herself, imagining him sprawled out on the sofa watching a baseball game, alternately shoving handfuls of dill pickle potato chips in his mouth and taking long swigs of low carb beer, pausing during commercials to pick the crumbs out of his chest hair and admire the growing collection of empties beside him. He probably doesn't even miss me, Eileen thought. He's probably loving the time to himself without me around to nag him to get off the couch and do something.

Eileen sighed, heavily. She wasn't lying when she'd told Cody she thought winning the trip was a turning point in her and George's relationship. Last summer, she and George had been sitting on a patio in Hamilton, arguing, when a young couple carrying a clipboard and a camcorder approached them. They said they were putting together a promotional video for the city, asking people off the street to share what they most liked about Hamilton. Anyone who participated automatically qualified to win the grand prize — an all-inclusive weekend trip for two to Montreal.

Eileen remembered being surprised when George agreed to participate. Even more surprised by his response. Of course, the biggest surprise came a month later when she received a phone call informing her that George was one of the five finalists. At a formal dinner the following week, Eileen, along with a host of Hamilton dignitaries and their spouses, watched the videotaped responses of each finalist. She remembered spontaneously smiling when George's face appeared on the large screen. The sight of him sitting on the patio in Hess Village immediately brought her back to that magical moment, the moment he looked into the camcorder and started saying things even she hadn't known. Things like how it had been his plan as a young man to walk across Canada before starting a job that was waiting for him in Vancouver; how he had every intention of following through with this plan until, seventy-four days after leaving Halifax, he caught sight of Eileen on the Bruce Trail in Hamilton; and, how, after spending the summer accompanying Eileen on long walks in and around the city, he knew two things: that he would marry Eileen and that they would remain in Hamilton forever.

After it was announced that George had won the grand prize, he and Eileen were immediately showered with congratulations and praise. Most of the women and even some of the men present couldn't stop commenting on what a romantic first encounter they'd had, that it was just like something out of an old movie. Eileen had felt wonderful, and, for a time, she and George returned to their old ways — hiking all over the city on the weekends, going out to dinner, making love. They even stopped seeing their marriage counsellor. Then, a little more than six months ago, things slowly went back to the way they were before —

"So, tell me, Eileen. What do you think of Montreal?" Jacques asked, interrupting her thoughts.

Eileen shrugged, "I don't know," she said, drearily. "I haven't seen that much of it."

"That is a shame. If you like, I offer you my services as guide."

Eileen chuckled. "Really?"

"Yes. But, I must warn you, I intend to show you a much different Montreal."

Eileen blushed. She wondered what her children would say if they could see her. Especially Cody. He was such a romantic, such a believer in true love and marriage and doing whatever it takes to remain together. Both of them, she was sure, would be shocked to hear what she was about to —

"So, we are agreed?" Jacques inquired.

For the first time since he had removed his sunglasses, Eileen noticed how handsome Jacques was, how his high cheekbones and mocha-coloured skin were a perfect complement to his soft, brown eyes. Eileen took a few moments to make it appear as though she may decline Jacques' invitation then nodded her head. "We are agreed," she replied, smiling.

"Good. But first, we must get rid of your other guide," Jacques said, motioning to her purse, then holding out his hand for Eileen to give him her guidebook.

When Eileen handed it to him, he sniffed haughtily at it, regarding it as though he were sizing up an unworthy opponent before calling over the waitress. *"Dans la poubelle, s'il vous plaît,"* he said, handing her the book.

"What did you say to her?" Eileen asked after the waitress had taken the guidebook from Jacques and retreated inside the café.

"I ask her to put it in its rightful place."

"Where?"

"The garbage, of course."

Eileen laughed. "So, what's next?"

"Next, we leave," Jacques said, standing up.

"Here? Why?"

"You have the same café in Hamilton, yes?" Jacques asked, pointing to the Second Cup sign.

Eileen nodded. Jacques shook his head, wagging his index finger at Eileen in mock disappointment. "Why come to Montreal? To sit in the same cafés you have in your own city? *Non.* That is not right. I always tell my customers to try new things. Experiment. In my bistro, we are always experimenting. That way, no one gets bored. It should be the same for you, yes?"

"Yes," Eileen said, smiling.

An hour later, they were in the heart of Old Montreal, strolling along Rue Saint-Paul.

Along the way, Jacques had played the role of tour guide, pointing out the various sites for her — Hôtel de Ville, Château Ramezay,

Notre-Dame Basilica — setting them in context, commenting on their architecture and significance while touching on the history of Montreal itself, its religious beginnings, the role that both the British and the French had in its construction, the enduring political tensions, the city's resurgence in the last decade as a cultural tourist mecca.

As she walked alongside Jacques, her eyes obediently following the direction of his knowledgeable finger, Eileen found herself smiling uncontrollably, charmed by Jacques' warm, luxurious voice and the scenery he was narrating — the cobbled streets, the coterie of cafés and bistros bulging with patrons, the ancient mansard roofs and rustic façades of the innumerable boutiques and galleries offering an enticing contrast to the *chic, au courant* merchandise contained within.

"I feel like I'm in France," Eileen said, pausing to read the name of the shop they were about to enter. "Or, rather, what I imagine France looks like."

"You have never been?" Jacques said, looking shocked, his hand resting on the shop's door handle.

Eileen shook her head. "I've always wanted to, but, well, my husband and I were content to stay close to home."

"I see. Perhaps we should discuss this during — oh, *pardon. Madame. Monsieur. Après vous,*" Jacques said, nodding and opening the door to *Les Délices de L'érable* for a couple about to enter the shop.

. . . . To Be Continued . . .

well, that too . . . .

"I can't believe you're still with her," Josette said, smiling appreciatively at the man still holding the door for her and Craig.

"Hey, it's not *that* hard to imagine, is it?" Craig replied.

Josette laughed. "Yeah, actually. It is."

She had met Craig twenty years ago during Winter Carnival in Quebec City. She was a waitress. He was a university student on vacation. One hour after the bar closed they were a couple. Three months after that, they broke up. Despite the brevity of their relationship, they'd kept in contact all these years. Whenever someone (usually a current boyfriend) would ask why she still spoke to him, she would smile and say, "He taught me to celebrate every inch of my body."

Craig believed that every woman has an Achilles' heel, an aspect of her body she loathes — big hips, small breasts, a crooked nose, thin hair, bad skin, a double chin, knobby knees; whatever it might be, this perceived fault can be the source of eternal obsession and debilitating depression.

For Josette it was her butt. Since turning fourteen she'd regarded it as though it were a separate entity, as though it had no business being part of her. The rest of her was so petite, so proportional, so polite. Then, as soon as one's gaze slipped past her waist, this enormous, bulbous bottom reared rudely up, its imposing size and shape soliciting unceasing commentary and curiosity from those around her. As a result, she became incredibly conscious of letting it out in public and took to wearing concealing clothes — long sweaters and shirts, slimming dresses and skirts, anything to reduce or hide its sizeable impression.

14

Craig, however, had changed all this. He loved her big butt. Adored it. Couldn't get enough of it. He encouraged her to walk around naked whenever they were alone, getting her to parade up and down imaginary catwalks just so he could watch her butt move. He even took her shopping and bought her several tight, form-fitting pairs of jeans, insisting she leave the long sweater at home. Then he took her to a club and urged her to dance, to confidently and proudly display her booty for the world to see.

Their break-up had been her idea. She'd blamed it on the distance, that it had become too much to travel back and forth between Quebec City and Toronto. Of course, this wasn't true. The real reason was she'd noticed a change in Craig. A few weeks after she began to feel confident about her body again, he began to withdraw, slowly phasing himself out of her life. Josette knew it would be only a matter of time before he moved on.

In subsequent years, Josette had come to realise this was Craig's *modus operandi*, that he sought out women with 'problem parts' and then set about trying to change their impression of those parts. Within a few weeks, three months at the most, he had women throwing out their Prozac and self-help books, refusing to watch *Dr. Phil*, cancelling appointments with psychologists and plastic surgeons, and celebrating every inch of their bodies.

Which is usually when he left. As soon as he was convinced a woman was honestly confident in herself, that the problem part was no longer a problem, he would offer his services to some other woman. Of course, like any good counsellor, he kept contact with his previous 'partner-patients,' making follow-up phone calls and visits just to be sure they were doing okay. But he never remained with one woman longer than a few months.

Which was why it intrigued Josette immensely that Craig had been with the same woman now for over two years. She was dying to find out more about this woman.

"So, what gives?" Josette said, now browsing the enticing array of desserts — *mousse bananerable, gateau au fromage, Charlotte aux fruits, tartelettes d'érable et noix* — ensconced behind the glass counter display of the dessert shop.

"What do you mean?"

"How come you're still with her?"

He smiled. "She's given me something that no one else has."

"What? A really long list of things to fix?"

He laughed. "Well, that too."

"Then what else?"

"Well, it's —"

"A baby!? Oh my God, you're having a baby?"

. . . . **To Be Continued . . .**

your heart will melt . . . .

Slightly embarrassed by the turning heads and temporarily suspended conversations in the small shop, Francesca smiled sheepishly at the man and the woman now looking at her belly, before turning to her friend, Rochelle, and nodding.

"Congratulations!" Rochelle squealed, throwing her arms around Francesca and giving her a hug. "Welcome to the club. You must be so excited!"

"Thanks. I am."

"How far along are you?"

"A little over three months."

"Three months! Why haven't you told us sooner?"

"We wanted to be sure. They say the first trimester is always, you know, iffy."

"Have you had your first ultrasound?"

Francesca nodded.

"Are you going to find out if it's a boy or a girl?"

"Um, I don't know."

"Oh, you really should find out. It doesn't hurt to —"

"Maybe she doesn't want to know," Marianne said, shaking her head at Rochelle, before taking a healthy bite of her *tartelette*.

"And maybe she will," Rochelle snapped back, giving Marianne a disparaging look — both for interrupting her and for taking such an obviously too-large bite of her tart. Then, returning her attention to Francesca, she said, "As I was saying, it doesn't hurt to have some advance notice. That way you can plan. Buy the right clothes. Get advice from other mothers who have raised a boy or a girl. Plus you can get the baby room all ready and don't have to do everything neutral or redo it later."

"Unless the ultrasound is wrong," Marianne quipped.

"You mean that can happen?" Francesca asked.

Marianne nodded. "It happens all the time. Doctors tell the parents they're going to have a girl, the parents go home and paint the baby's room pink, buy all girly clothes, and then, on delivery day — surprise, it's a boy! Trust me, Frannie, you're better off waiting."

"Don't listen to her," Rochelle sniffed. "She's just being her usual difficult self."

Francesca smiled politely at Rochelle. "Well, even so, I still think I'd like it to be a surprise. At least for now."

"Oh, don't worry," Rochelle said, patting Francesa's hand. "You'll have plenty of time to change your mind. Any names picked out?"

"A few. My mother bought us one of those name books ages ago hoping we would —"

"Oh, my God. Your mother!" Rochelle squealed. "I almost forgot about her. What did she say? She must be so thrilled."

"We haven't told her yet."

"She doesn't know?" Rochelle asked, looking slightly shocked.

Francesca shook her head.

"Why not?"

Francesca sighed. "We've been meaning to. It's just that, oh, I'm afraid she'll drive me crazy. I'm afraid that as soon as I tell her I'm pregnant, she'll either be calling or over at our house every day."

"I can relate," Marianne said, retrieving a few errant crumbs of *tartelette* from the corner of her mouth with an exaggerated swipe of her tongue, causing Rochelle to shudder. "My mother drove me absolutely bonkers my entire pregnancy. I should've moved away for nine months, come back and said, 'Here, say hello to your grandson.'"

Francesca chuckled. "Ever since Paulo and I got married my mother has told me she wants to be in the delivery room holding my hand when I give birth to our children. Can you imagine?"

"Why do they always want to do that?" Marianne said, shaking her head.

"I don't know what you two are talking about," Rochelle said, looking slightly offended. "I had my mother in the delivery room and it was great."

"Really? I don't think I could do that with her there."

"I'm with you all the way on this one, Frannie," Marianne said. "There are just some positions you don't want your mother to see you in. And this is definitely one of them."

"That's exactly what I think. But how do I tell her that without hurting her feelings?"

Marianne shrugged. "Maybe give her the 'Mom, I've got some good news and some bad news' routine."

"I don't know if that would go over so well."

"In that case, my only suggestion is to get it all sorted out *before* she finds out you're pregnant. And make sure you get it in writing."

"I hope Paulo is going to be there for the delivery, at least," Rochelle said.

"He said he would. For as long as he can handle it."

"Weak stomach?"

Francesca nodded. "He's terrified of the sight of blood."

"Are you going natural or C-section?"

"I don't know. I haven't decided yet."

"Do the C-section. That's the way I went. It's so convenient. You just book your appointment and poof, before you know it, it's done."

"Don't you miss out on a lot, though?"

"Only hours and hours of excruciating labour pain."

"Don't listen to her," Marianne said, frowning at Rochelle. "I had an epidural and I was perfectly —"

"Oh, dear. Now that you're pregnant, you really shouldn't be eating that," Rochelle said, pointing at the half-eaten *gâteau du chocolat* on Francesca's plate.

"What?" Marianne said. "Why shouldn't she?"

"It's not healthy for her baby," Rochelle replied, not bothering to look at Marianne.

"Yeah, well, if you listen to David Suzuki, neither is breathing the air, but you're still doing it."

Ignoring Marianne, Rochelle placed her hand firmly on Francesca's. "You should really watch what you're eating now. I ate nothing but organic foods when I was pregnant with Brittany. I didn't drink. Didn't go anywhere near cigarette smoke. No junk food. No processed, hydrogenated, or trans-fatty foods. No aspartame. Just wholesome, organic, healthy foods and environments."

"I was just the opposite," Marianne said, waving her hand dismissively at Rochelle. "I ate all kinds of junk food when I was pregnant."

"Really?" Francesca said, wriggling her hand out from underneath Rochelle's.

"Uh-huh. I mean, I always made sure I took the necessary vitamin and mineral supplements, but I also ate loads of chocolate bars, poutine, Big Macs, bacon, Diet Coke, jelly beans — and ice cream. My God, I must have eaten four litres of ice cream a week during my final trimester. It seemed as though every day I came in here and had some ice cream. I couldn't get enough of it. I mean just *look* at it over there," Marianne said, pointing to the decadent arrangement of designer ice creams displayed behind the curved glass counter. "I mean, who in their right mind would want to deny themselves *that*?"

"Who in their right mind would want to do *that* to themselves?" Rochelle asked, looking at Marianne as though she were a crazed lunatic.

"Do what?"

"Eat all that junk food while they were pregnant."

"To prepare my child."

"Prepare him? For what?"

"For what he's going to encounter on a daily basis once he goes to school. At least by that time he'll have built up a tolerance to it."

"That's irresponsible."

"No it's not. It's practical."

Rochelle let out a faux-laugh. "How is that practical?"

"Well, let's see. You haven't fed Brittany anything but organic, non-sweetened foods now for two years, right?"

"Right, so?"

"So, what exactly do you think is going to happen when she goes to her first birthday party and has a slice of the birthday cake? Or when she goes to daycare or kindergarten and trades lunches with someone? She's going to go into toxic shock."

"I think you're highly exaggerating," Rochelle snapped.

"Am I?" Marianne snapped back.

The two women glared at one another, their mouths twisted into scowls, their eyes hurling obscenities, until, as though both of them suddenly realised the same thing, their demeanour abruptly changed, their faces softening as they turned to look at Francesca.

"Oh, Frannie," Marianne said, taking hold of Francesca's hand. "We're so excited for you. Really, we are."

"You must be so happy," Rochelle added, taking hold of her other hand.

"Just wait until you see your baby for the first time."

"Or when she smiles for the first time."

"Or when he takes his first steps."

"Or when she first says, 'Mommy.' Oh my God, your heart will melt right there on the —"

"Would you please *shut up!*"

. . . . **To Be Continued . . .**

other firsts

It was what Gil wanted to scream at the three women. He didn't, of course. He just couldn't bear to hear this type of talk. Unfortunately, it seemed to be all he heard nowadays — in stores, at work, on the streets, on the radio, on TV. It was everywhere. People loved to talk about their kids.

He didn't.

It was one of his many regrets.

Another was not spending more time at home, and, when he was at home, not spending more time with his son.

Lately, however, he'd been trying to convince himself this was a blessing — his rationale being that the less memories a person had, the less painful the separation was. Case in point: his wife. She was in far more pain than Gil for the simple reason that she had far more memories than he did. She was the one who had been with their son twenty-four hours a day for the first four years of his life; she was the one who had witnessed all the milestones, all his firsts — his first smile, his first cold, his first tooth, his first steps, his first word, his first big-person meal — all the things that Gil had missed for one reason or another.

Staring down at the steam rising from his coffee, Gil methodically removed the piece of protective cardboard lining the paper cup. Setting it aside, he carefully wrapped his right hand around the cup. Within moments the heat was biting into his fingers and palm, scalding his skin.

Of course, Gil had been there for other firsts. The first hospital visit. The first appointment with the specialist. The first time he heard the specialist utter the word, 'leukaemia.' The first round of chemotherapy. The first time he saw his son's body laying in the open casket at the funeral home.

Gil tightened his grip on the cup. The coffee surged towards the rim, the steaming brown liquid slowly slurping over the edge and down the sides of the cup, streaming over his hand, wrist, and forearm, soaking into the sleeve of his dress shirt, immediately staining the white fabric.

"*Pardon, monsieur.*"

Gil looked up, in the direction of the voice. A man was holding out several napkins.

"For you," the man said, nodding towards Gil's hand.

"Oh. *Merci*," Gil said, taking the napkins and beginning to wipe off his hand and wrist and the counter.

"You're very kind."

. . . . **To Be Continued . . .**

do you have a cell phone?

"It was nothing," Jacques said in response to Eileen's comment, holding open the door to the shop for her as she exited.

"What do you suppose was wrong with him?" Eileen asked when they were outside.

"I am not sure. He seemed very . . . troubled."

Eileen nodded. She took a moment to replay the nice gestures Jacques had made in the last few minutes — opening the door for the young couple, getting a gift for a friend in the shop, retrieving some napkins and handing it to the troubled man. "You have a nice way about you, Jacques."

"*Merci*, Eileen. You do, too."

Eileen smiled. "So, where is it you're taking me?"

Half an hour later they were seated on a small rooftop *café-terrasse* that offered an uninterrupted view of the Old Port and the St. Lawrence River.

From the moment Jacques ordered them a bottle of wine until it arrived a few minutes later, Eileen remained in a near trance-like state — the combination of the savoury aroma of several spicy Franco-Caribbean dishes sizzling on the nearby open-air grill, the late afternoon sun lightly massaging her skin though the mesh parasol, the sensuous sounds of jazz being piped in from several recessed speakers and the soft breeze brushing over the rooftop all providing a provocative accompaniment to the breathtaking vista.

"This is better than your Second Cup, yes?" Jacques said, eventually, as though reading her mind.

Eileen smiled. "Much better. Thank-you."

"*C'est mon plaisir*," Jacques replied.

"How did you know about this place?"

"The same way you know. I was invited by someone who has been here. Only those who are invited are allowed to invite others."

"Really?"

"It is true."

"Well, I guess that means I can invite someone, right?"

"Of course. But only someone special."

"Is that what I am?"

Jacques took a sip of his wine. "We would not be here if I thought otherwise."

Eileen blushed and looked away, taking notice of the other patrons for the first time since their arrival.

An older gentleman and his much younger companion were tucked into the far corner, their hands and legs entwined, oblivious to the outside world as they studied the menu; a middle-aged couple dressed in formal evening attire were enthusiastically dining on mango and banana glazed duck breast, curried lamb, and puréed sweet potato, alternately sipping wine, smacking their lips, and smiling at each other; two younger men, dressed in casual summer attire, were bowing their heads and lifting their wine glasses in the direction of an older gentleman wearing a fedora, as though paying homage to him; and, finally, two women, holding champagne flutes, were staring wistfully at the spectacular view of the St. Lawrence River.

The entire scene — the view, the private *terrasse*, the open-air grill, the music, the carafe of Chardonnay and basket of bread on their table, the fusion of cultures, cuisine, and clientele — was, Eileen had to admit, *très romantique*.

She couldn't believe she was here. Was she really here? Was she really about to have dinner with a man she'd only met a couple of hours ago? Was she really sipping wine on a private *terrasse*? George hated wine.

Eileen encouraged him to try it, but he always refused, telling her wine was for women and wimps. Jacques, however, had seemed the picture of masculinity as he inspected the wine list, so confident and capable, eventually making a selection that he said Eileen would surely enjoy. And, of course, he had been right. She loved it.

Reaching for her glass, she noticed her dinner plate had suddenly sprouted a small, decorative gift bag.

"*Un petit cadeau*," Jacques stated, smiling.

"For me? But I thought you said this was for a friend."

Jacques smiled. "It is. *C'est pour vous, mon amie.*"

It was the same bag she had seen him receive in the shop they'd gone into. They hadn't been in the shop much more than a few seconds when a man had called out to Jacques, coming out from behind the serving counter to give him a big hug and a kiss on the cheek.

Jacques introduced Eileen to Alain, the manager.

"So, Eileen, what do you think? Do you appreciate our little shop?" Alain had asked, gesturing enthusiastically to their surroundings.

Eileen had smiled and told Alain it felt as though she'd just walked into autumn in the Quebec countryside.

"*Bon*," he replied, nodding with approval at her description. "That is the desired effect."

Moments later, after a brief exchange with Jacques in French, Alain declared, "*Un moment*. I have just the item," and disappeared into the back of the shop, beyond the glass partition where the shop's goods were being made. A few minutes later, Alain had reappeared with the gift bag, handing it to Jacques and refusing to accept payment for it.

"What is it?" Eileen asked, still staring at the package.

"You must open it to find out."

Smiling, Eileen carefully picked up the bag, holding it by the handles. It felt heavy. Solid. She swayed the bag gently from side to side.

"*Non*. No cheating," Jacques stated, waving a finger at her. "*Ouvrez-le.*"

Eileen set the bag back down on the table. While pulling out the ornate tissue paper, she noticed her hands trembling slightly and took several slow, deep breaths in an attempt to calm herself.

Inside the gift bag were two bottles. The first bottle — tall, slender, and curvaceous — contained a few hundred millilitres of 100% organic Quebec maple syrup. The second bottle — short, squat, and ornately glazed — contained a blend of maple syrup and spices, suitable for use as salad dressing or for marinating.

"They're beautiful," Eileen said, lightly caressing the bottles with her fingertips.

"*Comme toi,*" Jacques replied.

Eileen lowered her head. "Thank you."

"Ah, but, I must warn you. They are not for show," Jacques said, pointing at the bottles. "You do not put them up on a shelf to have something pretty to look at. *Non.* They are to be consumed. Alain would not have it any other way. He asked that you contact him to let him know what you thought of it. *Donc,* as soon as you are back in Hamilton, you must use them and then give him a call."

Eileen smiled. "I will."

"Promise?"

Eileen nodded.

"*Bon.* Now, have you decided on what you will take for the meal?" Jacques said, motioning to the menu.

Eating was the last thing on Eileen's mind. Her stomach had been fluttering since they'd left Second Cup. It reminded her of the first few dates she'd had with George. Each time they went out for dinner she'd order a full meal and not be able to eat a third of what was on her plate.

"Oh, I don't know, Jacques. I'm not very hungry."

"But you must have something to go with the wine, *non?*"

Eileen smiled politely. "Well, I guess I could have a salad."

"*Une salade? Mon Dieu,*" Jacques replied, rolling his eyes and shaking his head. "That is not a meal." And then, leaning forward and flicking his eyes in the direction of the open-air grill behind Eileen, he added, lowering his voice, "It would be a great insult to the chef if you only ate a salad."

Eileen glanced at the chef, then at Jacques, then at the menu, then back at Jacques. "I wouldn't want to order something extravagant and not be able to finish it."

Jacques smiled. "*Pas de problème*. This place," he said, gesturing at the *terrasse*, "it is open very late. We have all night to finish." Then, just as he was about to take a sip of wine, Jacques abruptly pulled the glass from his lips as though he'd just realised something. "Perhaps I am mistaken, Eileen. Perhaps you are in a rush to leave?"

"Oh, no. No. Not at all, Jacques. Really. No. It's not that. It's just that I'm, well, I'm . . ." Eileen stammered, trying desperately to think of some reason why she shouldn't order a meal. "It's just that I'm on a —"

"Please," Jacques said, immediately holding up his hand, motioning for Eileen to stop talking. "Do not tell me you are on a diet."

Eileen shrugged, nodding her head.

"*Quelle horreur*," he said, setting down his wine glass and placing both hands over his ears. "Diets are blasphemy to a chef's ears. Atkins. South Beach. The Zone. All of them. Blasphemous. And," he added, raising his voice slightly, "in this place, they are strictly forbidden. *Complètement Interdite!*"

Eileen looked around at the other patrons to see if they'd heard what Jacques had said. It seemed everyone was far too wrapped up in their own worlds to have noticed.

"Besides," Jacques was now saying, once again picking up his wine glass, "you are not in need of a diet."

Eileen chuckled.

"Why do you laugh?" Jacques said, frowning. "It is true. You have a beautiful figure. Maybe, a little too thin for me, but, who knows? A few good meals and we see. *D'accord?*"

Eileen smiled at Jacques. He was looking expectantly at her, his unrelenting almond eyes twinkling. "Well, if you insist."

"I do," he coaxed. Then, reaching across the table and gently taking her hand, he said, "Eileen, Montreal is a place for extravagance, for allowing the body to experience all the great pleasures of being alive."

Eileen allowed herself to receive the enticing embrace of Jacques' gaze for only a moment before letting go, choosing instead to focus on their joined hands. His thumb began gently massaging the inside of her wrist, making tiny circles and figure eights. The delicate friction from his touch sent sensuous shivers up her arm. Eileen felt a flush of colour rush into her cheeks. She stopped breathing.

"*Mes excuses*," Jacques said, in response to Eileen abruptly withdrawing her hand from his grasp, "I did not mean to offend."

Eileen, her eyes still on her hand, where his hand had been, tried to speak, to reassure Jacques that it was alright, but nothing came out. A few moments later, after having a sip of wine to steady her nerves, she raised her head and looked at Jacques. She could see he was concerned, that he believed he may have spoiled their chance at a lovely dinner.

Eileen reached over and gently squeezed his hand to reassure him that he had not. "You are right, Jacques. I am being silly. What would you suggest?"

Twenty minutes later, they had consumed the first two courses of the *degustation* — vegetable cream soup and caramelized Porcini mushroom slices bathed in a bowl of guava sauce — both of which Eileen had managed to enjoy almost as much as she enjoyed the sight of Jacques enthusiastically sniffing and tasting the food, confessing to deriving an almost carnal satisfaction from a well prepared meal.

Halfway through their second bottle of wine, Eileen began to feel much more relaxed. Encouraged and emboldened by Jacques' affection towards her, she decided she'd like to get to know him a little better.

"So, Jacques," she said, after taking another sip of wine. "Tell me about yourself."

During the next few minutes, as they sipped Chardonnay and started in on their *plats principauxs*, Eileen listened to Jacques tell her how he had moved to New Orleans from France at age twenty-two, found work as a busboy in a local restaurant, graduated a year later to waiter, then bartender, then sous-chef, then head chef, before eventually purchasing his own place exactly ten years after arriving in the United States.

"Now, *c'est mon raison d'être*," he concluded, referring to his bistro.

"So, you never tire of being alone?"

He shrugged. "I am rarely alone in my business. Besides, now, when I take my vacation, I always make sure I meet someone like you."

"Like me?"

"Yes. Someone who is full of passion. Someone who is ready to try something she has only dreamed —"

At that moment, Jacques stopped speaking and gave Eileen a puzzled look.

"What is it?" she said, her hand instinctively covering her mouth, thinking she may have some food stuck on her teeth.

"Do you have a cell phone?" Jacques asked, pointing at her purse.

Eileen heard the ring. "Oh, my, yes. My son gave it to me for this trip," she said, beginning to rummage through her purse. "He was worried when he found out I was going by myself. He works for Bell Canada. Here it is," she said, pulling it out of her purse. She stared at it for a moment. "Oh, heavens, I don't even know which button to push."

Jacques reached across the table and pushed the SEND button.

"Thank you," Eileen said. "I'll just be a minute." And then, turning slightly to her right, she put the cell phone to her right ear. "Hello?"

. . . . To Be Continued . . .

see you at the wedding

"Mom! Hey, how are you? . . . You are? Come on, really? . . . No, of course there's nothing wrong with that. I just didn't think you'd be, you know, doing so well because this was like the first time you'd ever been somewhere alone . . . You're not? . . . Who's Jacques? . . . I see. New Orleans, huh? Well, I hope you don't, you know, do anything you're going to regret or — oh, shit! Shit! Shit! Shit! You idiot! Damn it! What? . . . Nothing. Listen, Mom, I've got to go . . . I just do . . . I'm fine, really. I'll call you back in, I don't know, like, an hour or so, okay? . . . Okay, well, say 'Hi' to Jacques from New Orleans for me and be good, Mom. Dad misses you . . . I just know he does. Okay. Gotta go . . . I will. Bye."

Cody hit the END button on his cell phone, carefully slipping it into his front shirt pocket before pounding the dashboard, hard. "Damn it!" he shouted. Then, taking a moment to check his hair in the rear-view mirror and pop a fresh piece of chewing gum into his mouth, he added, "She'd better be worth it, Cody," before yanking on the door handle and stepping out of his car.

The owner of the parked SUV Cody had just ever-so-slightly rear-ended had already come out of the West Town Bar & Grill, quickly crossed the street, and was now standing between his SUV and Cody's car, scowling and shaking his head while surveying what Cody surmised was purely cosmetic damage.

"What the hell were you thinking?" he shouted at Cody the instant Cody stepped out of his car.

"Um, yeah. Listen, could you just hang on for a minute?" Cody replied, "I'll be right back." And then, without waiting for a response from the man, he began running down the sidewalk, heading north on Locke Street South.

"Hey! Buddy! Where the hell are you going?!" the man shouted after him.

A few seconds later Cody was standing in front of a woman even more captivating than he originally thought she was when he first noticed her. It was her eyes. They gave her a mischievous, mysterious aura. As though she knew more than she was letting on. Much more. It was the same way Cody thought Lauren Bacall looked when she was younger, the smouldering gaze a harbinger of tempestuous eruptions. For a moment, Cody considered using this as his opening line, telling the woman she looked like Lauren Bacall — a young Lauren Bacall in a tight black lycra halter dress — but then he reconsidered, thinking she might not know who Lauren Bacall was.

"Hi," he said, smiling, opting for the more traditional approach.

The woman did not respond. Instead, she continued looking across the street, as though unaware of Cody's presence.

"Um, yeah, okay," Cody stammered, feeling his confidence waning. "Well, this may seem like an odd question, but did you see what just happened over there?" he asked, pointing in the direction of his car.

Still not looking at him, the woman started to say something, then hesitated.

"Don't worry," Cody said, placing his right hand on his heart. "I promise I'm not going to have you subpoenaed as a witness or anything. I just want to know if you saw what happened."

When the woman nodded, Cody smiled. "That was because of you," he said, beaming.

"Because of me?" the woman replied, her gaze now firmly fixed on Cody, a mixture of confusion and doubt creasing her forehead.

Cody nodded. "If you weren't standing here I wouldn't have been desperately trying to get a second, third, and fourth look at you instead of watching where I was driving. And I certainly wouldn't have rear-ended that parked SUV over there."

The woman smirked. "You're going to have a difficult time convincing a judge it was my fault."

"A judge is the least of my worries," Cody replied, gesturing to the SUV owner who was now standing with his hands on his hips, glaring menacingly at Cody.

The woman chuckled. "He seems upset."

Cody nodded. "That he does. But you know what would make going back over there and talking to him a whole lot easier?"

"What?"

Leaning closer to the woman, as though he were about to share an intimate secret with her, Cody half-whispered, "If you said yes to meeting me for a drink tonight."

"It would, would it?"

"Very much so."

Smiling, the woman took a small step away from Cody and started sizing him up. A moment later the SUV owner shouted at Cody that it was a crime to leave the scene of an accident.

Cody put his hands together in mock-prayer. "You see what I'm going to have to deal with?"

"Tell you what," the woman said, tucking a phantom strand of hair behind her ear. "I'll be on the patio of Second Cup in Westdale Village at 9:30 PM. I'll wait for exactly ten minutes. If you're there, we can have a coffee together. If you're not, I hope the guy calls the cops and your insurance rates triple."

Cody beamed. "Awesome. I'll be there. Thanks. Oh, by the way," Cody said, offering the woman his hand, "I'm Cody."

"Pleased to meet you, Cody. I'm Jenna."

"Jenna, huh? I like that. You ever heard of Lauren Bacall?"

Jenna nodded. "She used to be married to Humphrey Bogart, right?"

"That's her. Anyone ever said you look like her?"

Jenna shook her head. "You're the first."

Cody smiled. "I love being the first," he said, starting to walk away. Then, stopping, he turned back to face her. "By the way, how long do you plan on standing here?"

Jenna shrugged. "I don't know. A few minutes. Maybe more. Why?"

"Well, it would really be great if you waved back at me."

"What do you mean?"

"You'll see," Cody replied, starting to jog in the direction of his car.

A minute after shaking hands with the upset SUV owner and introducing himself, Cody discovered the man's name was Karl and that he and his wife and some friends were having dinner at the West Town when one of his friends saw a car smash into the back of his SUV.

"'Smash' is a pretty harsh word," Cody was now saying. "It was more of a nudge, really. I mean, look at your bumper. There's not even a scratch on it. All the damage was done to my car — and that's only a couple of small scuff marks."

"So, why'd you take off like that, then?"

Cody smiled. "I was hoping you'd ask. I know it must have seemed a bit odd. You see that woman standing over there?" Cody asked, waving at Jenna who, after hesitating for a second or two, waved back.

Karl nodded. "What about her?"

"Well, even though up until a few minutes ago I never knew she existed, something tells me that she's the one. And, yeah, I know you're probably thinking I'm crazy. And I don't blame you. My mother and sister are always telling me I'm a hopeless romantic. But I've just got a feeling like this is it. You ever have that? You must have had that with your wife, right? No? Really? Well, see, ever since my sister and I were kids we've had to listen to my father tell us how he met my mother. Granted, it's a pretty cool story. But, if this woman and I end up together, I think I'll at least have a story that competes with his. And that's where you come in, Karl. You see, it's a tradition in our family that anyone responsible for the bride and groom meeting are invited to the wedding."

A few minutes later, they had exchanged full names, phone

numbers, and were in the process of shaking hands again.

"Be sure and call me if this changes," Cody said, pointing to Karl's business card before getting into his car and starting it up.

"Will do," Karl replied.

"Oh, and tell your wife I'm sorry I interrupted your dinner. She's a lucky woman. She's got herself one heck of a guy."

"Thanks."

"See you at the wedding," Cody said, crossing his fingers.

"Good luck," Karl replied, waving at Cody as he pulled away from the curb.

After taking a moment to reread the name and phone number on the card Cody had given him, Karl glanced at the woman Cody was hoping to one day marry, then slipped the card into the back pocket of his trousers before quickly crossing Locke Street.

Re-entering the lobby of the West Town, he paused for a moment, thinking of what he could tell his wife and friends, wanting to preserve the rather odd encounter he'd just had for himself, to keep it from his —

"Karl?"

. . . . To Be Continued . . .

Robert! . . . .

"I'm sorry. I didn't mean to scare you, honey," Emily said, reaching out to her husband. From the table in the restaurant she'd seen him standing in the foyer, talking to himself. Fortunately she'd been the only one. "I was just coming out to see if everything was alright with the car," Emily said, putting her arm around him and gently rubbing his back.

"Everything's fine," Karl said, smiling at Emily. "He barely nudged me. As usual, Scott was exaggerating."

"No damage then?"

Karl shook his head. "Not to ours. And there was only a scuff or two on his front bumper."

"Did he say why he hit you?"

"He did. Bit of an odd story, actually."

Emily waited for Karl to continue, for him to begin telling her what had happened. She knew he wouldn't, however. Not without prompting. It was how Karl was acting lately, refusing to volunteer anything, as though his thoughts and feelings and the incidents of everyday life had suddenly become classified and Emily's access to it increasingly forbidden.

"Well?"

"Well what?" Karl said.

"Aren't you going to tell me the story?"

"Oh. Right. He was trying to kill a bee."

"A bee?" Emily said, regarding her husband with more than mild suspicion.

Karl nodded. "Apparently he's allergic to bees. Swells up like a balloon and goes into anaphylactic shock if he gets stung. He said he has to carry one of those kits with him wherever he goes. Anyway, a bee flew in his open window and he panicked. He was trying to get it out, lost track of where he was going — and that's when he bumped into our car."

"Is that why he took off running down the street?"

"Huh?"

"To get away from the bee?"

"Oh. No, he said he knocked his wallet off the dashboard and out the window when he was swatting at the bee. He was just going back to get it."

Emily had seen the young man getting out of his car, saw him start running in the opposite direction after saying something to Karl, then stop in front of a woman wearing a black lycra halter dress, chatting briefly with her before jogging back to talk to Karl. Not once did she see him bend over to pick up a wallet.

Emily scrutinized Karl's expression for any hint of deceit.

There was none.

"What's that look for?" Karl asked, frowning at Emily.

"Nothing," Emily replied, smiling and once again rubbing his back. "You were right. It is an odd story."

Karl shrugged. "Ready to go back in and join the others?"

Emily nodded.

Karl opened the door for Emily and they walked inside.

"Hey, there he is," Brian said, pointing at Karl. "We thought we'd lost you. Everything okay with the car?"

Karl gave the gang — Brian, Brian's wife Debbie, Scott and his girlfriend Mya — the thumbs up as he and Emily slid back into their seats. "Everything's A-OK," he said.

"Good. It's your turn," Brian said, slapping him on the back.

The 'gang' had been going out for dinner as a group one Saturday

a month for over fifteen years now, rotating restaurants and cities —
from La Luna and the West Town in Hamilton to The Rude Native
and Mother Tucker's in Burlington, to the Cornerstone and St.
George Arms in Caledonia to Scaramouche and Senses in Toronto —
alternating the venue for their discussions which were sometimes
light, sometimes cerebral, and always entertaining. At least to them.

The one exception to this fifteen-year tradition was Scott's girlfriend, Mya. Just another in a long list of girlfriends Scott had asked
to accompany him, this would be Mya's seventh dinner with the
group. Two more and she would have the record.

"Are you guys sure it's my turn?" Karl asked, glancing around the
table.

"Positive," Brian replied.

"And it has to be good," Mya added. "You have to make up for
Scott."

"Hey, what was wrong with my topic?"

"You mean aside from it being boring and banal?"

"What are you talking about? *Seinfeld* was the —"

Tuning out Scott and Mya, Karl smiled to himself, thinking that
Debbie was right, it probably wouldn't be that much longer before
Scott was bringing someone else to their Saturday night dinners.

"I'm really going to miss her," Debbie had said to the others before
Scott and Mya arrived.

"Me too," Emily agreed.

"Who knows," Brian said. "Maybe he'll stick with her?"

"Not a chance," Debbie replied. "She's too smart for him."

"Why do you think he does that?" Brian wondered.

Debbie chuckled. "You mean date women smarter than him?"

"Yeah."

"*He* probably doesn't think they're smarter."

"Oh, come on. He has to."

"Hey, he hasn't realised it yet, has he? I mean, how long has he been
with Mya now, seven months?"

Moments before Scott and Mya had walked through the door of

the West Town, the four of them placed bets as to when Mya's "Last Supper" would be. Brian had her hanging in until Christmas, Karl until Halloween, Emily said she'd last until August, and Debbie, although she really hoped she was wrong, put her money on tonight being Mya's final appearance.

"What's the wager?" Brian asked.

It was agreed that whoever won the bet be allowed to select where they ate dinner for the next three outings.

Taking a moment to wink at Emily — both as a way of trying to get her to stop regarding him so suspiciously and as a way of saying, 'Uh-oh, here they go again,' referring to Scott's and Mya's bickering — he suddenly snapped his fingers. "I've got one."

"Alright," Brian said, enthusiastically clapping his hands together, effectively silencing Scott and Mya. "Let's have it, my man."

Clearing his throat, Karl leaned slightly forward in his chair. "If you could be anyone for the next few days, who would you be?"

The question generated a few smiles and a round of appreciative nods until Brian got things rolling by saying he'd want to be Houdini.

"Hmmm," Debbie said, bringing a finger to her lips. "I think I'd have to go with Tiger Woods. Or Bill Gates. No, I'm sticking with Tiger."

"Myself," Scott said, matter-of-factly.

"Anyone but Scott," Mya said, shaking her head at Scott.

Moments later, after the rest of the gang's gaze had drifted in Emily's direction, she smiled, coyly, at Karl and said, "I'd want to be Karl."

As expected, her response immediately set in motion a chorus of "oohs" and "ahhs" from the gang as well as a "Sounds like someone is being a little too secretive for his wife's liking" comment from Scott and an "I'm not so sure I'd want to be inside *his* head" comment from Brian. Then, after everyone had settled down, Emily posed the question to Karl, who said he'd want to be Henri Jacobin, prompting Scott to ask, "Who the hell is Henri Jacobin?"

After taking a slow sip of his beer, Karl, adopting a slightly regal tone of voice, said, "Henri Jacobin is a forty-one-year-old plumber diagnosed with D.I.D."

"What's D.I.D. again?" Scott said, double dunking a celery stick into his blue cheese.

"Dissociative Identity Disorder," Mya replied. "It's the not-so-new term for Multiple Personality Disorder."

Karl smiled at Debbie, who was giving him a "See, I told you she was smarter than he was" expression. "Apparently," Karl said, "when the psychiatrists interviewed him this Henri Jacobin fellow had more than fifty alter-egos."

"Fifty?" Debbie said, twirling her dyed blonde hair around her index finger, something she did whenever she was trying to decide whether or not to believe what she'd just heard. "That's a lot."

Karl nodded. "I know. And, apparently, he was adding more every few days. The whole thing was quite elaborate. He'd created an entirely different set of parents, relatives, siblings, friends, co-workers, and acquaintances. In fact, before he got caught, he was well on his way to rewriting his entire history."

"That's bizarre," said Emily. "With a capital B."

"Really?" Mya said. "I was thinking it was pretty normal."

"*Normal?*" Scott snickered. "How can you say he was normal?"

"I didn't say *he* was normal," Mya replied. "I said *it* was pretty normal, meaning his *response*."

"His response? To what?"

"Life."

"Life?"

Mya nodded. "Yeah. It was probably just a coping mechanism."

Debbie laughed. "Spoken like a true lawyer," she said, winking at Mya. "You plan on representing him?"

Smiling, Mya took a small sip of her vodka cooler then shook her head. "Dissociatives aren't really known for their fiscal capacity."

"Wait a second here," Scott said, sounding slightly annoyed. "When you say, coping mechanism, do you mean, like, this guy is sitting there thinking, 'Oh my god, I can't handle life' and instead of going on a coffee break or playing a round of golf or taking a vacation like most people, he starts inventing alter egos?"

Mya shrugged. "At least he didn't decide to run amok with a meat cleaver or sit up in a bell tower shooting people with a high-powered rifle."

"So you're saying that since he didn't kill anyone, acquiring a multiple personality disorder is a legitimate method of coping with life?"

Mya laughed. "Well, I'm not so sure a person can *acquire* a personality disorder the same way you can acquire a Gap T-shirt or a Volvo, but sure, why not?"

"Why not?" Scott said, throwing up his arms in exasperation while looking around at the others as if to say, 'Can you believe this chick?' "For starters, Mya, we've already got almost everyone under the age of forty-five totally immersed in virtual reality — and now you're proposing we take it one step further and have people start creating imaginary lives with imaginary friends and family and —"

"I had an imaginary friend once," Karl said, rejoining the conversation. "When I was eight."

"Now why doesn't that surprise me?" Brian said, smiling.

"He . . . he was interesting."

"Was?" Brian replied. "You mean he's not still around?"

Karl shook his head. "When I was nine my parents took me to Jamaica for spring break and he ended up staying there."

Brian chuckled. "Smart guy."

"He was, actually."

"Still keep in touch?"

"No, unfortunately, we don't."

"Not even a postcard at Christmas?"

Karl shook his head. "Not even that."

"Isn't that always the way?" Brian said, laughing. "You take someone to a nice vacation spot and they end up —"

"People, people, can we get back on topic, please?"

"Sorry, Scotty, my boy," Brian said, looking slightly bemused. "I didn't realise we were still in school."

"That," Scott said, sternly, waving his finger at Brian, "was not even remotely funny."

"Relax, I was just joking, bud," Brian said, grabbing the pitcher of beer and topping up Scott's glass. "So, where were we?"

"I was about to say that I can agree we all cope in different ways, but, I mean, come on, we're not talking about having an imaginary friend when you're eight years old. We're talking about someone who at the rate he was going would've had enough people to populate a medium-sized town in a few years. This is not something we should be encouraging."

"Why not?" Mya said. "I mean, at least he's being creative. At least he's not just sitting on a couch being entertained and amused by TV or video games, content to exist in an imaginary world created for him by others."

"That's not my point. Whether it's someone else creating an imaginary world or Henri Jacobin, it's still an imaginary world. It's not real. And I can't believe any of you would seriously advocate multiple personality disorder as a healthy, well-adjusted method for expressing creativity."

"Well, if I had a choice," Karl said, "I think I'd rather live in a world of my own creation than someone else's."

Brian clapped his hands together loudly before raising both his arms in the air as if he was signalling a football player scoring a touchdown. "I knew it," he said, bringing his hands down and pointing both index fingers at Karl. "I knew the reason you picked this topic was because you admire the guy."

"Who?"

"Henri Jacobin. You admire him, don't you?"

"Who wouldn't?" Mya said, answering for Karl. "Come on, Brian. Think how fun it would be. I mean, most of us don't have a say in what our name is going to be, let alone where we're going to live, who will raise us, what our ethnic background will be, what our religion will be, where we'll go to school. It's all basically predetermined for us.

Now, here's an opportunity to reinvent all this. Think about it. If you could do it all over again, who would you want to be? Would you want to be male or female? Homo, hetero, or bisexual? Where would you want to live? What would you want your name to be?"

There was a temporary vacuum of conversation while each person mulled over the possibilities until everyone, in unison, suddenly shouted "Robert!" the moment Karl's cell phone started playing Rick James' song, "Superfreak." As a way of letting him know who was calling without having to open his cell phone and look at the call display, Karl had programmed everyone's phone number into his cell phone to correspond with a different song — in this case, "Superfreak" for his friend and business partner, Robert Cairns.

Scooping the cell phone off the table, Brian quickly opened it and hit the SEND button.

"Hey, Robert . . . Yeah, it's Brian . . . Good, you? . . . Great. Listen, I was just wondering who you'd want to be for a few days if you could be anyone . . . Yeah, anyone at all . . . Ha. Nice one."

"What'd he say?" Debbie asked.

"He wants to know if he can be more than one person," Brian said, causing everyone to start laughing.

"Huh? . . . Yeah, sure. Here he is," Brian said, handing the phone to Karl.

"Hey, Robert," Karl said into the phone. "I'm just going to head outside so I can hear you better, okay? . . . Yeah, hang on one second."

Getting up from the table, Karl mouthed the words, "Be back in a minute" to Emily before heading for the exit.

"So, what's up, Robert?" he said as he stepped outside. "Hmmm? . . . No. Not really . . . Yeah, we're just having our regular Saturday night dinner . . . At the West Town . . . Yeah, it's not bad . . . No, no. That's okay. I can spare a few minutes. What's on your mind?"

. . . . **To Be Continued . . .**

flatlined . . . .

"I'm really sorry to bother you, Karl, but I was wondering if you're not busy later on, maybe after dinner you could . . ."

Robert stopped short of finishing his sentence, waiting for Karl to do it for him, to offer to come over. That way he wouldn't feel guilty. That way he could always say, 'Hey, I didn't tell you to come over.' A few seconds later Karl asked if he wanted him to come over.

"Yeah," Robert replied. "But, I mean, only if you want to . . . Of course. I understand. You think she'll say it's okay? . . . True enough. Alright. Well, I'll be here. So, you'll call me back as soon as you talk to Emily then? . . . Great. Thanks, Karl."

Robert hung up the phone and sighed. He sincerely doubted Karl would call back and tell him he was coming over, not when he was already out with the 'gang.' "Besides, who would want to hang out with me in this state?" he said, sweeping some cracker crumbs off the couch and onto the carpet with the back of his hand.

He glanced at the TV. It was muted and set to the TV guide channel. He'd been watching it this way for most of the day, unable to decide on a program. The majority of the floor, table top, and counter space in the four-bedroom house he'd bought five years ago in Ancaster's Meadowlands had become a repository for all kinds of paraphernalia: old newspapers, empty juice containers, beer bottles, pizza boxes, opened DVD cases, fast-food cartons, candy wrappers — evidence of the gloomy turn his life had taken in the past few months.

Robert guessed it was around February when he began noticing his patients were considerably healthier than he was. At first he thought

50

it might just be a case of seasonal affective disorder — the February blahs — but when spring arrived a couple months later with the sun firmly in tow and his mood still didn't improve, he knew it was something more serious than a simple bout of S.A.D.

By early June, he'd began documenting his symptoms.

"I don't feel things the way I used to," he'd said into his voice recorder during a break between clients. "Nothing excites me anymore. Nothing makes me sad. Nothing makes me angry. I keep thinking I should be feeling this or that under these circumstances, but I'm unable to do so. Instead, I just feel numb. All the time. It's as though I'm merely going though the motions of my life. Pretending to be alive."

When a person exhibiting these symptoms presented himself to Robert in his office, he usually diagnosed the person with unipolar depression and recommended weekly counselling sessions to get at the underlying cause or causes of the person's condition.

What was interesting about Robert's condition, however, was the fact that it had seemingly developed without an underlying cause. There was no definable incident or crisis responsible for triggering it. No divorce, no death of a significant other, no loss of job, no change of career. Nothing.

"It's as though my feelings have completely flatlined," he'd told Karl a few days earlier. "As though every emotion I used to have has been replaced by a general malaise."

Despite turning to Karl, Robert knew Karl wasn't his best chance at a recovery. Karl had his own issues. Issues that, in Robert's professional opinion, if left unchecked, could have more disastrous ramifications than Robert's current condition. It was just that Karl, being his partner, was his most readily available and least expensive avenue of assistance.

After getting up from the couch, Robert took a moment to steady himself, resting his hand on the nearby plant stand. He felt nauseous. It was the first time he'd been vertical since early this morning. Although today was still only Saturday, he was quite confident he would not make it into the clinic on Monday.

He began thinking of the effort it would require, pondering the sheer number of steps involved in making this a reality. There had to be dozens, possibly hundreds.

First the alarm goes off at 5:45 a.m., he thought. Then I hit the SNOOZE button once. When the alarm goes off a second time, I hit the OFF button and roll the summer duvet cover off. Then I get out of bed. Make the bed. Grab a towel out of the linen closet. Turn on the portable stereo unit in the bathroom. Tune in to CBC Radio One. Have a shower. Decide while showering what cologne to put on. Apply cologne and deodorant after showering. Decide while shaving what suit to wear. Return to the bedroom after shaving. Select the suit. Put on socks, shirt, and trousers. Leave the suit jacket and the tie on the bed. Return to the bathroom. Gel and style my hair. Wash my hands. Return to the bedroom. Put on the tie. Carry the suit jacket to the kitchen. Drape it around the breakfast table chair furthest from the dishwasher. Open the refrigerator. Grab a bottle of Evian water. Take a sip. Pop a multi-vitamin. Take another sip. Walk to the front door. Select a pair of dress shoes to match the suit. Put them on. Return to the kitchen. Retrieve the cell phone, car keys, and wallet from the kitchen counter. Ensure that there are enough business cards in the wallet. Slip the cell phone into the inside pocket of my suit jacket, then the car keys and wallet into my trousers. Take another —

Robert sighed, loudly. "Christ, I haven't even made it out the front door yet," he said, collapsing back on the couch.

When the phone rang a minute or so later, Robert stared at it for a few rings, knowing it was Karl, knowing Karl would tell him he wasn't coming over, knowing that this would mean he would have to resort to —

. . . . **To Be Continued . . .**

I'm married

"Hey Robert . . . Well, I just spoke with Emily and she said the gang had planned on seeing a movie tonight after dinner . . . Yeah . . . Um, well, after the movie we were planning on going to go back to our place for drinks . . . Yeah, so I don't think I can make it tonight. But, hey, you're quite welcome to join us at the movie theatre or at our place later for a drink . . . You sure? . . . Well, call me if you change your mind. Alright. Talk to you soon."

Karl hit the END button on his cell phone and breathed a huge sigh of relief. He wasn't in the mood to listen to his partner whine about his emotions having flatlined or how bland his food tasted.

Slipping the cell phone into his front shirt pocket, Karl was about to head back to the West Town when he heard a car horn honk and then someone, a man, shout, "How much?!"

Turning in the direction of the noise, he saw two young men in a silver BMW, one of them hanging out the passenger side window, gesturing at the woman Cody had been talking to earlier. The woman smiled and said something that Karl couldn't hear but which caused the driver of the BMW to brake suddenly and pull the car up alongside the curb just before Pine Street. The woman, now wearing sunglasses, sauntered seductively towards the car. After conversing briefly with the occupants, the passenger side door abruptly opened and she quickly climbed into the back seat.

"What's your story, lady?" Karl said, aloud, his hands on his hips as he watched the BMW pull away from the curb.

"You want the short version or the long version?"

When Karl looked in the direction of the voice, he saw a woman in what he guessed to be her late thirties to early forties seated on one of the benches outside the Locke Street Bakery.

"Excuse me?"

"You asked what her story was and I simply wondered if you wanted the short or long version?"

"Oh, I was actually referring to — do you know her?"

The woman nodded. "We're associates."

"Really?" Karl said, quickly scanning the woman's clothing — business jacket, pleated skirt, white collared shirt, high heels, small clutch purse — surmising, after including the pair of large, dark-rimmed sunglasses resting on top of shoulder length jet-black hair in his assessment, that she worked in an office, probably a law office. He often played this game with Robert, guessing what a person's occupation was based on their attire. "What line of work are you in?"

The woman gestured for Karl to come closer and when he did, she whispered, "We're escorts."

Karl righted himself immediately. "Is that so," he said, trying to sound nonchalant while taking a step away from the woman.

The woman nodded. "We just started working Locke Street yesterday," she replied, crossing her legs and repositioning the skirt on her knees. "Normally we service the downtown core but we've been branching out lately, trying to service different areas — the east end, the mountain, Ancaster, Dundas. We were even in Burlington for a while until some jealous housewives got together and chased us out. So far I really like it here. Lots of traffic. Nice restaurants and cafés. Easy to pretend we're window shopping for antiques instead of cruising for potential clients when a cop drives by. And they even have these lovely benches so we can sit down when our feet get tired."

Karl, now making a quick visual scan for a police cruiser, was thinking of a tactful way to excuse himself from the conversation.

"So, what are you into?" the woman asked.

"Excuse me?" Karl said, looking slightly perplexed.

"S&M? Bondage? Oral?"

"I'm not —"

"My associate, the one you were asking about, well, she pretty much does it all. But you're going to have to wait. She probably won't be back for an hour, maybe more."

"I —"

"Of course," the woman continued, uncrossing her legs and smiling suggestively at Karl, "if you prefer the company of a more *experienced* lady, I'd be more than happy to entertain you."

"I'm sorry, I'm not into that sort of, I mean, thanks, but I prefer, I'm actually —"

"I should've known," the woman said, recrossing her legs and adjusting her skirt. "You look like the type who prefers the younger ones. Well, like I said, she should be back in an hour or so. You can wait with me, if you like," the woman said, sliding over a few inches on the bench and patting the empty space beside her.

Not waiting for Karl to respond, the woman sighed, heavily. "It's always the way, isn't it?" she said, gazing down the length of Locke Street. "No one values experience anymore. Everyone's so preoccupied with youth. Especially in this business. I told my associate she'd better enjoy it while she can. Time has a way of catching up to a person, I said, and before you know it you'll be spending most of your money on expensive clothes and surgery so you can look young again."

The woman chuckled. "Naturally, she told me this would never happen to her — which is precisely what I used to say. Until the customers started complaining. Then I changed my tune. I got my breasts done two years ago and my lips done last year."

Pausing to push out her chest and pout her lips, the woman batted her eyes a couple of times at Karl before pointing an immaculately manicured finger at him. "I'll warn you right now, though, she's as naive as she is beautiful. Every time she sees a BMW or a Lexus or some other fancy car pull up she thinks it's going to be the man who will fall madly in love with her. She has '*Pretty Woman* Syndrome.' By the way, what kind of car do you drive?"

"I'm sorry, I don't mean to be rude, ma'am. But this has nothing to do with your age or me desiring a younger woman. I'm married," Karl said, pointing to his wedding ring.

The woman smiled. "Oh, that doesn't mean much in our business," she said, waving her hand dismissively at Karl's ring. "We treat wedding rings like a watch or a pair of cuff links. It's just another accessory."

"Well, I treat it very seriously," Karl replied. "Again, I don't mean to be rude but I really should be getting back to my dinner. With my wife."

The woman smiled. "Suit yourself. If you change your mind, you know where to find us."

"Thanks. But I don't think that will happen."

. . . . To Be Continued . . .

well, then, what is it? . . . .

"Poor bugger," Suzanne said to herself, watching the man nearly running back to the West Town and flinging himself through the entrance. "That'll teach you for wanting to know what a woman's story is."

Smiling, Suzanne took a moment to review what she'd said to the man, somewhat impressed with the story she'd been able to fabricate. "I guess all that time I spent Internet dating is finally paying off," she said.

She hadn't fabricated everything, mind you. She really did like Locke Street. It had undergone quite a facelift in recent years, transforming itself into one of the trendiest little neighbourhoods in Hamilton. And one of the busiest. Especially on the weekends. Sliding on her sunglasses, Suzanne made a series of quick mental snapshots of her surroundings, alternately aiming her lens at the splurge of young fashionistas boldly brandishing their exotic, up-to-the-second clothing and hairstyles surging past her; the wooden hydro pole pierced with hundreds, possibly thousands, of staples from past postings of CD release parties, community events, and lost kittens; the clump of casually clad lads cooing over a Porsche Boxster parked in front of a nearby gallery; the symmetry of the eight A-framed roofs on the north side of Tuckett Street; the luxurious scent of Paco Rabonne cologne originating from the middle-aged man with a Hawaiian shirt and matching canvas shoes seated on his Yamaha Virago motorcycle; the —

"Suzanne!"

Snapping her head in the direction of the voice, Suzanne saw her friend, Julia, on the other side of the street, waving at her.

"Been waiting long?" Julia asked, after they'd exchanged kisses and told one another how good the other looked.

"Barely five minutes," Suzanne replied.

"So," Julia said, taking a seat beside Suzanne on the bench. "Who was that?"

"Who?"

"That man I saw you talking to?"

"Oh. Just some guy."

"He was cute."

Suzanne smiled at Julia's hopeful tone, the look of expectancy in her eyes. "Yes, he was. He was very cute. And married. He and his wife are having dinner at the West Town."

"Really? That's too bad," Julia said, patting Suzanne's hand.

Suzanne nodded. "All the good ones are either taken or have an STD."

"Excuse me?" Julia said, giving Suzanne a "What the heck was *that* supposed to mean?" expression.

"Oh, nothing. Never mind," Suzanne replied. "Just an inside joke."

"Between who?"

"Me, myself, and I," Suzanne said. Then, pointing at Julia's blouse, she said, "Hey, this is nice."

"You like?"

"Very much. Is it new?"

Julia nodded. "Roger bought it for me. Can you believe it? The man has such great taste."

Suzanne smiled, trying to imagine the Julia of two years ago allowing a man to buy her clothes for her. So many things had changed.

"Where did he get it?"

"He wouldn't tell me. Probably Vancouver. Or Montreal. He's in both places every other week."

"Well, he certainly has an eye for fashion."

Julia nodded. "He continually surprises me," she said, smiling.

Then, pulling back a bit to survey Suzanne's outfit, she said, "Speaking of fashion, I really like what you've got going on here."

"I'm trying to capture that whole naughty-Catholic-school-girl-meets-classy-business-woman look."

"I think you've nailed it. And I love the sunglasses. Very Jackie O."

Suzanne smiled. "Thanks. So, how long do we have?"

Julia shrugged. "As long as we want."

"Really?" Suzanne said, glancing at her watch. She'd been hoping Julia would say they only had a couple of hours. That way she could get back to Toronto in time to see —

"I told Roger I was going out with my bestest friend and that he'd more than likely have to wait until the sun came up tomorrow before seeing my face again."

"Wow. That's great," Suzanne said, trying to sound excited.

"So, bestest friend, what would you like to do first?"

Suzanne shrugged. "Oh, I don't know. I thought I'd leave the social itinerary up to you."

"Well, in that case, I think our first order of business should be to have dinner. Nothing too substantial, mind you. We have to make sure we leave enough room for all the tequila poppers and vodka coolers we'll be having later on." Julia let out a short squeal. "Look out, Hamilton. The South Oval Sluts are on the prowl!"

Suzanne smiled. She hadn't heard that expression in a long time, not since before Julia's wedding. She and Julia had met during Frosh week at McMaster University, when they lived on the same floor in Brandon Hall. The following year they moved off campus, sharing a house with four other ex-Brandon girls on South Oval Drive in Hamilton's west end. Their house parties at Homecoming, Halloween, Christmas, and at the end of each school year were what gave university life its bad reputation. And its enormous appeal.

For Julia and Suzanne, the partying had continued after graduation, long after, as they went on frequent bar-hopping excursions to Montreal, Toronto, Kitchener, Niagara Falls, London, Buffalo — even New York City. Ten years after they'd graduated, they were planning to move to Toronto to take advantage of the more affluent entertainment scene when Julia met Roger, got married, and had her first baby — all within eighteen months. This would be the first time in nearly a year that Suzanne and Julia were going out.

"Hey," Julia said, suddenly, taking hold of Suzanne's arm. "Is everything okay?"

Suzanne looked at her friend. The last couple of years had opened up a gulf between them — not unbridgeable, just wide enough to make her hesitate. "I'm fine," she said. "Just a little preoccupied. I've got a few things on my mind."

"You want to talk about it?"

Two years ago Suzanne wouldn't have waited for Julia to ask if she wanted to talk about it, she would've just told her. Of course, two years ago Suzanne wouldn't have found herself in the predicament she was now in. And, realistically, she sincerely doubted Julia would understand.

"It's nothing, really. I probably just need a cup of coffee to clear my head."

Julia squeezed Suzanne's arm. "Want to grab one here?" she said, nodding in the direction of the bakery.

"Sure, why not," Suzanne replied, grabbing her purse and following Julia into the bakery.

The smell of toasted bagels and fresh brewing coffee immediately lifted Suzanne's spirits. "So," she said, walking towards the coffee dispensers, "how is little Alex?"

Julia smiled. "Not so little, anymore. He's growing like a weed."

"How old is he now?"

"He'll be four months on Monday."

"Wow. I can't believe he's already four months. Are you still breast-feeding him?"

Julia nodded. "I had to pump all day today to make sure Roger had enough for his feedings tonight. He started teething last week and so he's not sleeping through the night anymore which has been a bit of a strain on —"

As Suzanne continued half-listening to Julia talk about her baby, she thought of how much had changed in the past two years, how Julia had quit her job (something she said she'd never do), moved out of the city into the suburbs (also something she said she'd never do), got married, had a kid, and stopped social smoking (again, all things she said she'd never do).

Even though Julia always pretended to be envious of Suzanne, incessantly telling her she missed her single woman status, Suzanne was certain Julia wanted nothing more than for Suzanne to join the married-with-kid(s) club. Of course, Suzanne knew Julia would never say so, and not just out of common courtesy. It had more to do with the fact that it had always been Suzanne's dream to find a man, get married, and have children before the age of thirty-three. Never Julia's.

It seemed so strange to hear Julia gushing about motherhood, talking about spit-ups, changing diapers, burping, and breastfeeding. Suzanne shook her head. Julia Caulfied and Motherhood. The two were incompatible. Mutually exclusive. Which is precisely what Julia used to tell Suzanne on a near monthly basis before she'd met Roger.

Of course, for Suzanne, the more incongruous change in Julia's life was the fact that she got married. Aside from telling Suzanne hundreds of times that she didn't believe in the institution of marriage, she also swore up and down that one man could never fulfil all her desires, let alone her moods.

It wasn't long after Julia traded in her many men for Roger that Suzanne adopted her friend's philandering philosophy, hurling herself into the weekend party scene, allowing herself to be wined and dined by multitudes of men in the hopes that one day, just like Julia, she would stumble upon her Roger.

"So, what about you?" Julia said, as they sat down on one of the stools at the front window, setting their purses and coffees on the counter top. "How's life in Toronto?"

"It's good. Great, actually. I really like where I'm living now."

"Where'd you move to again?"

"The Annex."

"You were on King West before, right?"

Suzanne shook her head. "Queen West."

After a few moments of semi-awkward silence and two sips of coffee each, Julia leaned over and nudged Suzanne. "So," she said, "how many men are you dating at the moment?"

Suzanne hesitated. She considered making up a number, a large number, just to appease Julia. "I'm not actually dating men."

"Oh, come on. You expect me to believe that? Dish the dirt, girl-friend."

"I'm serious. I'm not."

"Really?"

"Really."

"Hmmm," Julia said, looking at Suzanne as though she wasn't completely convinced Suzanne was telling her the truth. "Well, by the end of the night you will be. I'll make sure of it."

The last time they'd gone out, a month or so after Julia and Roger were married, Julia got really drunk and tried to set up Suzanne with nearly every guy in every bar they went to. Suzanne had spent the entire night alternately cringing with embarrassment and apologising to the men for Julia's behaviour. She wasn't looking forward to a repeat performance.

"You know," Suzanne said, smiling wanly, not wanting to dampen Julia's enthusiasm, "the truth is, I'm not really up for bar hopping tonight."

"You're not?"

"If you don't mind, I'd rather we just had a nice, quiet dinner somewhere."

"Okay. Wait a second, here. First you tell me you're not dating anyone. Now you're telling me you're not up for the bar scene. Where did the crazy party girl Suzy Chen go? Is she still in there somewhere?" Julia said, gently poking Suzanne in the ribs.

"What can I say, it's the new me," Suzanne replied, shrugging. "Besides, I didn't say I wasn't dating anyone, I said I wasn't dating *men*."

Julia's face scrunched into an expression of obvious confusion. She leaned in close to Suzanne. "So, um, wait," she said, her voice now a barely audible whisper. "When you say you're not dating *men*, are you saying you're . . . you're not saying you're a . . . I mean, you're not dating *women*, are you?"

Suzanne laughed and shook her head. "No."

"Oh. Well then, what are you saying?"

"I'm saying I'm dating a *man*. Just one. Not men."

Julia squealed and hugged Suzanne. "Oh my God. Why haven't you told me this? Who is he?"

"He's just a guy I met."

"Where?"

"Online, actually."

"Really? When?"

"Almost a year ago."

"A year? How long have you been together?"

"Ten months."

"Ten months? You have so been holding out on me, Suzy. I can't believe you. Why haven't you said anything?"

"I didn't want to jinx it."

Julia took a moment to regard her friend. "That's okay. I forgive you," she said, patting Suzanne's arm. "So?"

"So what?"

"So what's his name? What's he like? What's he do? Is he the one?"

Suzanne tried unsuccessfully to contain her smile. "His name is Thomas and he's amazing. He's caring, sensitive, and masculine. He loves jazz. We go to clubs and concerts all the time in Toronto and Montreal. He likes hockey and hiking. He's got a great job. A job that he loves. He's a creative consultant for a computer software company. He's brilliant. And . . ."

"And?"

"And he's younger than me by seven years."

"Seven? You go girl!"

"I know. He tells me all the time that me being older is a huge turn-on for him."

"That's great. And so, well, do you think he could, you know . . . ?"

"What? Be the one?"

Julia nodded.

"I don't know. We've got a few things to work out first."

"Like what? He sounds perfect."

"He is. Almost. There's just one not-so-small problem."

"Different religions?"

"No. We're both Protestant."

"He's not married, is he?"

"No. No. Nothing like that."

"Well, then, what is it?"

Suzanne scanned the bakery, checking to see if anyone was eavesdropping on their conversation. Satisfied that there were no straining ears, she leaned over and —

"Julia Caulfield?"

Suzanne turned to look at the woman who had just called Julia's name. Tall, pretty, thin, in her mid-thirties, and wearing a very expensive vintage pant suit, the woman looked as though she'd just walked off the cover of *Hamilton Magazine*.

"I thought that was you," the woman was now saying, setting her purse down on the counter beside Suzanne. "I was just walking by, saw you sitting here and thought I'd say hi. It's Kristan. Kristan Demolir. We met at prenatal class, oh, God, it must be what, seven or eight months ago now?"

"Oh, yes. Of course. I remember. Hi," Julia said, applying a fake smile to her face.

Julia had recognised Kristan immediately; in fact, she'd already replayed the scandalous story she'd heard from one of the other women in their prenatal class about Kristan Demolir and her pregnancy. Married, but obviously not happily, Kristan started having an affair with her sister's fiancé. A few months later, after discovering she was pregnant with her sister's fiancé's baby, she divorced her husband and married her sister's now ex-fiancé — all before her third trimester.

"So," Kristan was now saying. "How are you?"

"I'm good, thanks. You?"

"Fabulous. I finally lost all the weight I gained during the preg-nancy," Kristan said, striking a pose as though someone was about to take her picture. "I'm even a few pounds lighter than I was before."

Julia reapplied the fake smile. "You look great."

"Thanks. I'm actually on my way to Milli to buy a few new outfits to celebrate."

"Really? I've completely given up on buying new clothes. Every time I do, they end up being covered in spit-ups or smudges."

Kristan nodded. "I know. Thankfully, Jacobus does most of the feedings."

"So, you're not breastfeeding then?"

Kristan shook her head. "I decided it wasn't for me. Besides, Abby seems to really like her baby formula. And this way she and Jacobus get to bond."

"So you had a girl?"

Kristan sighed. "We were hoping for a boy. Girls are so much more work. I don't know how I'd manage if Jacobus wasn't such a hands-on father — and we didn't have our doula."

"What's a doula?"

"You haven't heard? They're like live-in nannies. Ours comes in after dinner, puts Abby to bed, and stays with her through the night. She'll feed Abby. Burp her. Change her diaper if she needs it. Comfort her if she cries. It's really great because this way Jacobus and I get a full night's sleep."

"Wow. That sounds —"

"Excuse me," Suzanne said. "I don't mean to —"

"Oh my God, I'm sorry," Julia said, interrupting Suzanne, placing her left hand over her mouth and her right hand on Suzanne's arm. "Where are my manners? Suzanne, this is Kristan. Kristan, this is my best friend Suzanne."

"Nice to meet you, Kristan," Suzanne said, offering Kristan her hand.

"Nice to meet you, too."

"I was actually just going to say that I have to leave for a few minutes," Suzanne said, sliding off her stool. "I've just got to make a quick phone call and then grab something from my car. I'll be back in a few minutes."

"Okay, we'll be here," Julia said before returning her attention to Kristan, who had already assumed Suzanne's seat. "So, tell me more about this doula person. Is she expensive?"

Spinning on her heel, Suzanne walked swiftly out of the bakery, heading south on Locke Street, in the opposite direction as her car.

"Unbelievable," she said, aloud, referring to the fact that Julia had completely forgot Suzanne was even there as soon as "Ms. I Have A Baby, Too" walked through the door.

Stopping in mid-stride, Suzanne considered going back into the bakery and telling Julia that she was leaving, that Julia and her new best friend, Kristan Demolir, could spend the evening comparing feeding schedules and diaper brands. "I knew this was a mistake," Suzanne said, under her breath. "I shouldn't have even agreed to go out with her tonight."

A moment later, Suzanne realised she was standing in front of the West Town. Looking inside, she caught sight of the man she'd been talking to outside the bakery. He was sitting with a small group of people, his arm around a mousy-looking brunette who Suzanne surmised was his wife.

Waiting until the man and his wife noticed her, Suzanne then smiled coyly at the man, giving him a flirtatious wave before she continued walking up the street. The West Town contained mostly bitter memories for Suzanne — unflattering images of her, *sans* Julia, joining the rest of the women-over-thirty crowd mounted on high heels and trying to young down their appearance by wearing low rise jeans, crop tops, and the most recent hairstyles in a desperate attempt to get some balding schlep with a beer belly and a goatee to buy them a drink and ask them out on a date.

At the time, Suzanne convinced herself she was having fun, that this was a necessary rite of passage for women her age, occasionally finding truth in Julia's adage that a women's many moods and desires required a buffet of men to satisfy. But then, after going home with a barely legal young man one night and overhearing him talking on his cell phone in her bathroom, telling one of his buddies that he was about to 'bed a cougar,' she realised she had to find an alternate method of finding a partner. Three years of Internet dating and dozens of bad dates later, she'd finally found herself a great guy.

Now standing at the corner of Locke and Chatham, Suzanne wondered whether she shouldn't just turn around and walk back to her car, drive to Toronto, and wait for Thomas to get back from Niagara Falls so she could tell him the great news.

"Suzanne!"

It was Julia, half-running towards her, waving. "I'm an idiot," she said when she reached Suzanne.

"Why?"

"Because I just abandoned you."

"What are you talking about? I had to make a call. Besides, you seemed like you were enjoying the conversation with Kristan."

"Please. The woman is a nightmare. I couldn't wait for her to leave."

"Why?"

"Well, to begin with she — no, forget about her. This was supposed to be our night. And you were just about to tell me something really important."

"Oh, it's okay," Suzanne replied.

"No, it's not. Please don't let me being an insensitive idiot prevent you from telling me."

Suzanne shrugged. "I've kind of lost my nerve."

"Listen, you don't have to tell me now. Let's just go somewhere nice, order some food, and talk about something else, okay? And if at any time you feel like telling me, you can just —"

"I'm thinking of having unprotected sex with Thomas."

Julia hesitated, looking confused. "Wait, is that what you wanted to tell me?"

Suzanne nodded. "Sort of. It's part of it."

"Um, okay. So, does this mean you're thinking of getting pregnant?"

Suzanne shrugged. "I'm not sure. We've talked about it. Quite a lot, actually. Thomas is all for it."

"Won't your parents be upset if you don't get married first?"

"Of course, they will. Especially my father, But that's not really what I . . . I mean, I'm on the pill now and I'd probably stay on it even if we were having unprotected sex. At least for a while."

"Oh. Well, then, what's the . . . I don't understand."

Waiting until a group of couples had walked past them, Suzanne leaned over and whispered into Julia's ear. "Thomas has herpes."

"Oh my God. Are you serious?"

Suzanne nodded.

"How long have you known?"

"Since I met him. He was really up front about it."

"And you still went out with him?"

Suzanne nodded. "Of course. There's more to a person than just that. Besides, it's not that big of a deal."

"But won't you get it?"

"Maybe. Probably. I guess it depends on when we make love. There are dormant phases. And he's taking medication that helps to control it."

"Is he pressuring you to do this, Suzy?" Julia asked, suddenly taking hold of Suzanne's arm, looking concerned.

"No. Of course not. It's something I want to do. For us."

"Oh. I'm sorry. It's just that, well, what if things don't work out between you guys? What if six months or six years down the road you split up and you're stuck with . . . ?"

"Don't you think I've thought of this? It's all I've thought about since Thomas told me. He's not perfect. But I've never been treated better or been with someone more honest in my life. He's exactly what I've always wanted."

"Minus the herpes, of course."

Suzanne felt herself getting annoyed. She was starting to regret telling Julia. "Unfortunately, I wasn't able to preorder my partner," she said, straining to control the hostility in her voice. "But when I compare Thomas to my last half dozen boyfriends, I think he's far better than any of those freakshows."

"Is that yours?"

"What?"

"The phone."

"Oh, yeah. Thanks," Suzanne said, reaching quickly into her purse and pulling out her cell phone. "It's Thomas," she said, looking at the call display.

"Well, say 'Hi' to him for me."

Suzanne smiled and hit the SEND button on her phone. "Hey babe, how are you?"

. . . . To Be Continued . . .

take a picture? . . . .

"Great. You? . . . That doesn't sound too convincing. I guess your friend Julia didn't take the news so well, huh? . . . Are you okay? . . . Is she standing right there? . . . Oh . . . Do you want me to let you go? . . . You sure? I probably shouldn't have called you anyway. I just missed you and wanted to know how things were going . . . It's the truth. Well, that and the fact that I need a break from my family . . . Yeah, we're still here. We just went on the Maid of the Mist boat tour a little while ago. I'm still holding my blue raincoat . . . No, unfortunately, I didn't see her . . . Well, even if I did, I'd still choose you . . . I'm serious. Lelewala doesn't even come close to your beauty . . . Yeah, my grandparents loved it. That's all they've been talking about . . . Some. I understand more than I can speak. Their English is pretty good, though . . . I know. I know. I still can't believe I'm in Niagara Falls. I feel like such a tourist . . . Um, probably another few hours . . . Yeah, we're just deciding where to have dinner and my parents still want to visit the casino so we probably won't get back to Toronto until midnight or so . . . I miss you, too. You still up for meeting my family tomorrow afternoon? . . . You sure? . . . Great. Well, I guess I should let you get back to your friend. Call me if you want, okay? . . . Okay. I love you, Suzanne. Bye."

"Was that her?"

Thomas jumped. "Mother!" he said, stuffing his cell phone into his pant pocket. "Were you eavesdropping?"

Helen smiled. "Maybe."

"Mother, you're —"

"I'm kidding. I was just on my way back from getting a water for your grandmother when I spotted you here," Helen replied, holding up a small bottle of water.

"Oh."

"So, was it her?"

Thomas nodded. "Yes. It was."

"Did I hear the word 'love' escape your lips, young man?"

"I thought you said you weren't eavesdropping?"

"I wasn't. I merely overheard a few words."

"Mother."

"Yes, dear?"

"I want you to promise to be nice to her."

"Of course. I'll be on my best behaviour. Still, for the life of me I don't know why you had to get rid of Nicole. She was such a catch."

Nicole was Thomas's last girlfriend. His mother adored her. Wealthy, beautiful, a shoo-in for a young Audrey Hepburn, Nicole was a part-time actress with a full-time penchant for physical experimentation that bordered on the extreme, often employing her body as a testing facility for a variety of radical research projects. This extremist behaviour had resulted in her contracting herpes while participating in an orgy at some semi-famous movie producer's condo in downtown Toronto, which she then passed on to Thomas.

He had been devastated by the news. Even more devastated when he found out Nicole had known she'd had herpes before they'd started dating. She seemed quite unimpressed by his devastation, however, telling him she thought it wouldn't really matter to him, that since he knew about her adventurous lifestyle and still wanted to be with her, he should have expected something like this.

"Besides," she'd said, perhaps as way of trying to console him, "having a sexually transmitted disease is all the rage these days. Everyone's either got one or is trying desperately to get one."

In those few short seconds, Thomas realised how much his life would have to change, that unless he adopted the same attitude as

Nicole, this disease would severely limit his dating options. And, should he ever decide to get married, he would no doubt have to settle for someone who wasn't nearly as attractive as he'd like her to be.

"So, what's she do for a living?" Helen asked.

"Mother, I thought we agreed. No advance notice."

"Why? What's the big deal? Why are you being so secretive?"

"I'm not being secretive. I just want you to make up your own mind about her. I don't want you to have a preconceived idea of what she's like."

"Well, am I allowed to know how you feel about her? Or is that a secret, too?"

Thomas thought about it for a moment. Well, for one thing, he thought to himself, she's older than I would've liked. At thirty-four, Suzanne wasn't one of these women who had the body or face of a twenty-seven-year-old. Years of late night bar-hopping, social smoking, a poor diet, and a rarely used gym membership had, if anything, made her look several years older than her real age. Of course, this was one of the reasons Suzanne was more inclined to overlook his condition.

"Well?"

"After taking a moment to consider your question, mother, I have concluded that my feelings regarding Suzanne will not be disclosed until the two of you have met."

"Scoundrel."

Thomas smiled. "Shall we join the others?"

"Where are they?"

"Just over there," Thomas replied, pointing in the direction of the Falls walkway.

His mother followed his finger. "Ah, yes. I see them," she said, taking his arm. "So, tell me, Thomas. Are you having any fun with us old fogies?"

"Actually, I am. It's bringing back memories of when we first came here," Thomas replied, picking his way through the throngs of people strolling along the walkway, leading his mother towards the spot where his father and grandparents were. "I was twelve, right?"

"You were thirteen," his mother corrected. "And you were the most incorrigible young boy on that trip. You pestered us relentlessly to let you go on the Maid of the Mist boat tour. You wanted to get as close as possible to the Falls. Do you remember any of this?"

Thomas shook his head. "Not at all."

Of course he remembered it. The night before they visited the Falls he'd come across the legend of Lelewala — the Maid of the Mist — in a tourist brochure. When he saw an artist's rendition of Lelewala he became instantly enchanted. It was the first time he recalled experiencing a simultaneous rush of desire and sense of loss. The brochure explained how the Seneca Indians would appease the Thunder God by sacrificing a maiden each year, sending her over the Falls in a canoe. According to the legend, one year, Lelewala, the most beautiful of all the maidens and daughter of the tribe's chief, was selected to go. On her way down the Falls she was caught by the Thunder God's two sons and, to this day, could still be seen hovering near the bottom of the Falls.

Thomas had never told anyone of his boyhood infatuation with Lelewala, keeping it a secret all these years, until yesterday, when he'd told Suzanne that he kept climbing the railing and leaning over to see if he could catch a glimpse of her, endlessly pestering his parents to take him on the boat tour, convinced he would be able to see her if he just got close enough.

"So, what do you think of your father's parents?" his mother said, interrupting his thoughts.

His grandparents had arrived three days ago, from the Ukraine. It was only their fourth visit to Canada. The first three visits they'd spent out west, in Calgary, where Thomas had lived the first thirteen years of his life. Thomas's father had immigrated to Canada in 1971, working for Esso during the oil boom of the seventies and eighties before moving to Toronto the year Thomas entered high school. It was the reason they'd visited Niagara Falls when Thomas was thirteen. His parents were scouting places to live in Southern Ontario and Niagara Falls — along with St. Catharines, Hamilton, London, and Toronto — was on the list.

"I think they're great," Thomas replied. "They seem a lot older than when I last saw them. But they're still in great shape."

"Yes, they are."

"I wish I could speak more Ukrainian."

"That's alright. Your father does a good job of translating. And their English is passable."

"I know. It's just that I'd really like to talk to them about the corrupt politics in their country in the past few years; you know, the assassinations, the rigged elections, the people demonstrating for weeks out in the cold just to have a fair election. Remember all that?"

His mother nodded, adding, with a slightly sarcastic tone, "I don't think your father's parents were out in the streets demonstrating, dear."

Thomas smiled. He was well aware of his mother's mild aversion towards her in-laws, especially her mother-in-law. "You and Baba seem to be getting along okay," Thomas said, referring to his father's mother.

"Yes, well, I find it easier to be nice to someone I only have to see once every five or six years."

"Mother, you're absolutely horrible."

"It's the truth! That woman put me through hell when I was engaged to your father. No one was good enough for her beautiful boy, especially not a no-good Irish woman like me."

Thomas had heard the story many times before, how his father's parents did not approve of the match, how they'd journeyed from Europe to Calgary in an attempt to change their son's mind, telling him they had a nice, full-blooded, Ukrainian woman back in the home country already picked out for him.

"But they couldn't stay mad at me after I had you," his mother said, squeezing Thomas's arm. "Not after I gave them a grandson to carry on the all important family name."

Thomas laughed.

"Okay," his mother said, tightening her grip on his arm. "Enough of this talk, here we —"

"Ah, there they are," Thomas's father said, gesturing to Thomas and his mother.

"Well, have we decided on dinner?" Thomas's mother asked.

"I think we're going to go with the buffet at the casino."

"Excellent. I'm starving. I'm not used to having dinner so late."

"So, how is everyone doing?" Thomas asked, smiling at his grandparents.

His grandparents both returned his smile and Thomas's father said, "Your grandfather was just saying how there must be tourists from dozens of different countries visiting the Falls today. He's never heard so many different languages in such a short span of time."

"Yeah, it's pretty amazing," Thomas said, joining the others in surveying the large, shifting tableau of visible ethnicities moving along the walkway until the sight of a petite Caucasian woman narrowed his focus. Standing by herself, her back to the nearby railing, she was looking expectantly at Thomas, as though waiting for him to answer a question. A moment later, when a sudden gust of wind tossed her long blonde hair into a frenzy, making her laugh as she tried hopelessly to tame it, Thomas couldn't help but think that this was the type of woman he'd like to —

"— take a picture?"

. . . . To Be Continued . . .

what were you thinking?

After a few moments of waiting for a response, Kalan surmised that the guy — judging by his confused, almost embarrassed expression — either hadn't heard him or didn't understand him. "I was wondering if you could take a picture?" Kalan said, again, this time a little louder and a little slower, restating his question while gesturing towards his camera. "Of me and my girlfriend?"

"Oh. Yeah. Sure. Of course," the guy said, sounding relieved, reaching for Kalan's camera. "Do I just point and shoot?"

"Yeah. It's that button right there," Kalan said, handing the guy the camera and pointing to the red button, before backing up towards Rhonda, "Maybe take three or four, if you don't mind?"

"Not at all."

"Oh, and can you try to get the rainbow in the picture?" Kalan asked.

The guy looked through the camera lens and nodded. "Just tell me when you're ready."

Kalan gave Rhonda a few seconds to get her hair under control and then gave the guy the thumbs up. The guy took four pictures then handed the camera back to Kalan.

"Thanks a lot," Kalan said.

"My pleasure," the guy said, quickly rejoining the small group he'd been with.

As Kalan tucked the camera back into the side pocket of his cargo shorts, his fingertips brushed against the small felt box already in his pocket. He looked at Rhonda. She'd turned around again and was now staring intently at the Falls. Kalan pictured himself getting down on one knee and calling her name. With his hand still in his pocket, he picked up the tiny box, and began turning it over and over in his hand.

There had been so many moments during the past two hours that he'd thought about proposing: in The Loveboat Restaurant during lunch; in Oakes Floral Theatre as they sat staring at the coins people had thrown in the water; in the Butterfly Conservatory — just before the Monarch had landed on Rhonda's shoulder. He'd asked the guy to take a picture of them just now because he finally felt he was going to do it and wanted to mark the occasion. Though he was certain Rhonda loved him and would probably say 'Yes!' with an exclamation mark, there was still a small seed of doubt.

"What are you thinking, babe?" he asked, in an effort to plumb her thoughts.

"You really want to know?" Rhonda said, still looking at the Falls.

"Yep," he replied, nodding and taking her left hand. "I really want to know."

Rhonda smiled. "Okay, well, as I was standing here, staring at the Falls, watching the falling water pounding against the water at the base and seeing the mist rising up and spraying us, it reminded me of when I saw the twin towers collapsing, how they pounded down-wards, crashing onto the street below, and how the smoke and dust and ash billowed up and out and rained down on everyone. Do you remember where you were when you heard about it or saw it for the first time on TV?"

"Of course. I was in my apartment."

"I was taking a course only a dozen blocks from Ground Zero."

"You were?"

Rhonda nodded.

"How come you never told me that before?"

She shrugged.

"So you were there? I mean, you actually saw everything?"

She nodded. "I was taking a three-day course with a bunch of other people from work and from where we were we could see the towers burning. A few minutes later, when someone rolled a TV in and we learned what had happened, the couple teaching the course got worried about not being able to catch their flight back to Maryland that evening and so they cancelled the test scheduled for the end of the day and told us they were going to pass all of us and that we'd receive our course certificates in the mail in a few weeks. As soon as we heard we didn't have to write the exam and we'd still be getting our certificate, everyone started cheering and clapping, until the man beside me said, 'I can't believe this. We're celebrating the fact that people are dying.'"

Kalan shook his head in disbelief. "That's horrible."

"I know. But even though I wasn't one of the people clapping, I still had no feelings for those people trapped in the towers. No sympathy. No connection. In fact, I was hoping there would be more attacks. I was disappointed when that plane didn't make it to the White House or the one that hit the Pentagon didn't do more damage."

Kalan looked around him, wondering if anyone else had heard what Rhonda had said. Aside from the people walking past them, the closest person to them was a middle-aged woman wearing a wrinkled turquoise blue sundress standing by herself with her eyes closed. Kalan hoped her hearing wasn't good. Or, if it was, that she wasn't a fellow American.

"Why were you disappointed?" he asked, turning back to look at Rhonda.

"Because I thought the attacks were deserved."

Kalan glanced at the middle-aged woman again. The mist from the Falls had speckled her sundress and was gathering on her slightly upturned face. A moment later, tiny rivulets of water began streaming down the woman's cheeks, making it seem as though she were crying.

"Deserved?" Kalan said, letting go of the box in his pocket. "Why?"

"Well, you know how the religious fundamentalists are always pointing to some calamity and saying it's God's wrath, that it's punishment for some evil or wrongdoing — like how they persecute gays and say that AIDS is an example of God's wrath, that He doesn't approve of this type of behaviour and so He created AIDS to get rid of it? Well, I was thinking that maybe all this terrorism is merely a reaction to all the evil things the U.S. has done to the rest of the world for the last sixty years or so. I mean, we don't exactly have a spotless record. We're the biggest supplier of arms in the world. We've supplied arms to both Iran and Iraq as well as to Saudi Arabia. We've set up dozens of militaristic regimes around the globe. We've bombed the hell out of Iraq under the false pretense of there being weapons of mass destruction. We deserve this treatment, we deserve to pay for our sins."

Rhonda stopped talking.

"Is that it?" Kalan asked.

Rhonda nodded.

"You sure you weren't thinking anything else?"

She smiled. "I'm sure," she said. Then, smiling at him, she asked, "How about you? What were you thinking?"

"I was thinking I would've liked to have been in one of the towers when it was hit," Elizabeth Brassard thought to herself, her eyes closed, trying in vain to prevent her tears from joining the tiny droplets of water already dribbling down her face.

. . . . To Be Continued . . .

or worse . . . .

"Why do you wish that?" Elizabeth pretended the young woman standing nearby asked.

"I lost both my children," Elizabeth replied.

Lost.

A euphemism.

Elizabeth hadn't lost them.

The truth was they'd both committed suicide.

Her daughter Jennie because she couldn't cope any more with the way people were treating the Earth. Her son, Ryan, out of guilt for letting Jennie die.

"Oh my God. That's terrible."

Elizabeth nodded. There wasn't a waking hour that had passed in the last few years when she didn't think of it, when the question, "Why?" didn't slam into her cerebral cortex, when the searing pain from having to bury her two children didn't plough into her heart, threatening to completely pulverise it. She would have given anything, anything at all — including her own life — to have saved even one of them. "It's the hardest thing a parent can ever do," Elizabeth said, her eyes now soaked with tears.

She'd moved back to Niagara Falls last year, settling into a small house on McLeod Road a couple of blocks from her childhood home on Brant Avenue. Until Elizabeth moved to Hamilton shortly after her eighteenth birthday, whenever something was really bothering her, she would walk down to the Falls. While standing beside the wall of water, leaning against the railing, she would close her eyes and allow the thunderous pounding to envelope her senses. Eventually, her troubles would subside or gain more context and she would be able to find some measure of understanding or peace. She had thought that by moving back here and once again being close to the Falls, it would do her some good, ease her pain. What she learned, however, was that even the Falls weren't capable of making some things better.

She and her husband had been on vacation when they received the news of Jennie's death. Elizabeth was mortified. Inconsolable. Her pain — so intense, so raw, so suffocating — had prevented her mind from forming words to describe what she was feeling. A deafening stillness settled into her heart, causing her to remain outwardly silent. Her husband was the opposite. He needed to talk about what had happened. He wanted them to get counselling, join a support group, and visit Jennie's grave site every week. Elizabeth couldn't even bear the thought of hearing Jennie's name. She'd sooner have someone hack off her right arm.

Their incompatible ways of grieving drove a wedge between them and she and her husband were separated only a few months after Jennie's suicide, divorced within the year. It was in this state — divorced, living alone, Jennie's death still a festering wound seemingly incapable of healing — that Elizabeth had received a package from her son, Ryan, containing a series of letters and a video tape.

Elizabeth remembered making herself a camomile tea and popping the video into the VCR. What she saw was beyond her realm of comprehension.

On the TV screen, Elizabeth saw Ryan, sitting in his bedroom at their family home in Hamilton, calmly watching a small video monitor. On the monitor was Jennie, lying naked in the bathtub down the hall. Moments later, Jennie began slitting her wrists while Ryan continued watching the monitor as his sister's blood filled the tub. A few minutes later, Jennie was dead. Stephen King could not have written a more gruesome or disturbing screenplay.

In near shock, Elizabeth immediately called her son, Ryan, shouting obscenities into his voicemail for several minutes. Only after she hung up the phone did she read the enclosed letter from Ryan, the one explaining what had happened, how sorry he was, that he was on his way to Lake Superior to, as he put it, 'mete out his penance.'

Elizabeth called the police, alerting them to her son's letter. A few days later, they found his body and confirmed what he had planned.

"What possessed the two of them to do this?" she'd asked herself a million times.

Elizabeth had read her daughter's suicide note and watched the video dozens of times, listening to Jennie say how disillusioned she was with the world, how she believed that only an insane species would wilfully put chemicals into the air they breathe, the foods they eat, and the water they drink. Only a species without compassion and foresight would spend billions on advertising to sell burgers and beer while millions of people starved and didn't have access to clean drinking water.

And then she would read Ryan's letter, read how he had thought he was doing his sister a favour, that he believed Jennie sincerely felt she was becoming part of the problem, and suicide was her only solution. In the end, however, Elizabeth took some solace in the fact that Ryan sounded terrified that he could've allowed such an atrocity to occur and appear so unaffected. His only explanation was that he was the logical conclusion to growing up in a world without limits, in a world increasingly immune to catastrophe and capable of viewing almost any behaviour as normal.

Before she left the house today, Elizabeth had sealed the letters and video in an envelope and placed it inside the already lit wood stove. She didn't want anyone discovering it and turning it into a cheap, sensationalised newspaper headline. Or worse, a cheap, sensationalised movie-of-the week.

Even before watching the video and reading the letters that first time, thoughts of her own suicide had consistently invaded Elizabeth's waking hours. Even now, as she gripped the railing overlooking the Falls, she was considering it.

There was nothing to stop her. She had no kids, no job, no friends, no husband. She'd heard from someone that her ex had put in for a job transfer and was now living in British Columbia. She regretted not opening up to him, sharing their grief, but had realised long ago that it was too late for apologies and second chances. Elizabeth knew there was only one escape from the haunting isolation inhabiting her soul.

Turning away from the Falls, her left hand still tightly gripping the rail, she opened her eyes and took a final look around, desperately searching for something to hang onto, a sight that might bring her back from the brink. A moment later she saw a couple seated in a horse-drawn carriage. Smiling and holding hands, they seemed genuinely happy. Elizabeth felt the compulsion to wave.

. . . . To Be Continued . . .

are you the owner?

"Harold, look," Candice whispered to her husband.

"Look at what?"

"At that woman over there," Candice said, nodding in the direction of a woman standing beside the railing overlooking the Falls. "The one wearing the turquoise blue sundress. She's waving at us like we're royalty."

"That's because we are, my dear," Harold said, affecting an English accent and returning the woman's wave.

Smiling at Harold, Candice joined him in waving at the woman. "I can't wait to tell the girls in the office. They won't believe this."

"I take it you're having fun then?"

"Oh, Harold. I'm having a wonderful time. Just wonderful."

Harold had surprised her two days ago at work, coming into the office on her morning break and inviting her outside where she saw their car was already packed and ready to go. He'd arranged the entire vacation, even getting her boss's permission for her to take the trip. They'd left Boston immediately, crossing the border into Canada and checking into their room at Howard Johnson's just before dinner. After dining at The Loveboat Restaurant, they'd decided to go for a swim and a sauna back at the hotel before retiring to bed early. This morning they'd strolled around Clifton Hill for a while, had a late picnic lunch in the park and then went on the Journey Behind the Falls tour before Harold had suggested they cap off a perfect day by taking a horse-drawn carriage ride.

"So, where would my princess like to dine tonight?"

"Oh, I don't know," Candice replied. "I hadn't thought that far ahead yet."

Since chatting with a fellow tourist from Boston, she'd been dying to try the buffet at the casino but knew she shouldn't suggest it; Harold would be too tempted to gamble. And drink. Yesterday, they'd celebrated Harold's third month of sobriety.

"How about we head up Clifton Hill and see if anything tickles our fancy up there?"

"Sounds good to me."

The carriage slowed. A car, a black Mercedes convertible, was illegally stopped on the street in front of them. Bringing the carriage to a halt, the driver informed Candice and Harold that she was not permitted to go around the vehicle since it was too dangerous. They would have to wait. "The car's engine is still running," the carriage driver said, "so it's probably just someone who wants to take a quick photo of the Falls."

Harold sighed and shook his head.

"That's okay," Candice said to the driver, quickly placing her hand on Harold's thick, tattooed forearm and giving it a gentle squeeze. "We can enjoy the view for a while. Right, honey?"

Harold smiled and patted her hand. "Sure."

Candice noticed he still had some automotive grease under a couple of his fingernails. Harold had been a mechanic for most of his life, occasionally working construction or on a demolition crew when he got laid off or was fired for not showing up after a night of heavy drinking.

"Hey, look. Two rainbows," Harold said, first pointing towards the Bridal Falls on the American side and then gesturing to the rainbow hovering over the Horseshoe Falls.

"Oh, Harold. They're beautiful," Candice said.

Harold nodded. "It sure is nice here."

"Even nicer than the first time we came here," Candice said, smiling.

That was almost thirty years ago, for their honeymoon. Long before

Harold's drinking became really bad. Before Candice knew he gambled. Before she knew he had a violent temper. Before he started hitting the kids. And her.

"Seems like a lifetime ago, doesn't it?" Candice said.

"At least."

Candice and Harold looked at each other and laughed.

"We've been through a lot together, huh?" Harold said, giving Candice a playful nudge.

She nodded. "We've seen our fair share, that's for sure."

They kissed, then turned to look at the rainbows again.

Candice's friends, the gals at the office, told her she was crazy to go back with Harold, saying he would cause her nothing but grief. Some of them reminded her of the tears, the bruises, the beatings, the nights she'd had to spend at their homes, fearing for her life. He might be able to hold himself together just long enough to get you back, they warned, but then he'll go right back to being his old self. Her mother wasn't buying the changed man theory, either. She didn't have any faith in his rehabilitation, believing the anger management classes he was required to take were a joke. Sooner or later, he's going to show his true colours, she'd said. And then you'll be sorry.

"This is ridiculous," Harold said, suddenly, starting to tap his feet while scanning the crowd in an effort to determine who the driver of the Mercedes convertible was.

"It's okay, honey. Really, it is."

"Can't they see we're behind them? There are signs all over the place."

"They're probably just trying to get some photos like she said," Candice replied, gesturing at the driver. "And who can blame them? It's beautiful here. Besides, we're not in a rush, are we?"

"I just wanted this ride to be perfect."

"It is, honey. If it takes a little longer, it takes a little longer. I don't mind. It gives us more time to see the sights."

Harold sighed. "You're right. I'm sorry."

Candice smiled, relieved that she'd been able to redirect him this easily. "I can't believe we're here, Harold," she said, squeezing his arm again. "In Niagara Falls, Canada. Tell me again why you did this?"

Harold shrugged. "I just wanted to do this as a way of saying — they're from New York."

"Huh?" Candice asked, giving him a puzzled look, even though she knew exactly what he was referring to. She'd hoped he wouldn't notice.

"The plates," Harold said, pointing at the Mercedes convertible. "They have New York licence plates."

"Oh, Harold. Come on now. I'm sure they're not Yankees fans."

The only thing Harold despised more than New Yorkers were Yankees fans, believing them to be a bunch of mental midgets for supporting a team he thought was directly responsible for trying to undermine the parity of America's favourite pastime. Sure, the Yankees were the most successful team in baseball history, but their owner also had the deepest pockets and was able to buy the best players. Which was why he was dumbfounded as to why anyone in their right mind would legitimately root for a team whose salary for only three or four players was more than many team's entire payroll. Of course, the fact that Harold had lost thousands of dollars betting for or against the Yankees at various times in the past thirty years was also responsible for his animosity towards the team and its fans.

"This has gone on long enough," Harold said, standing up in the carriage.

Candice cringed. She knew what was coming next.

"Would the inconsiderate asshole driving this imported hunk of illegally parked junk move it before I do it myself!" Harold shouted.

He was now scouring the crowd like a deranged lunatic, ready to pounce, his face crimson, the veins on his neck bulging, his powerful hands bunched into tight fists. Candice knew he was beyond consolation or redirection. Nothing short of the owner immediately appearing, apologising profusely, and moving the car right away would pacify him.

"Is there a problem?"

The question came from a young guy, probably no more than twenty, walking towards the convertible.

Typical, Harold thought, glaring at the young guy. Another spoiled rich kid thinking the rules of the road don't apply to him.

"Are you the owner of this vehicle?" Harold asked, barely able to rein in his hostility.

The guy shook his head. "He is," he said, throwing his thumb in the direction of two other young guys walking towards the car. One of them was wearing dreadlocks, the other, a Yankees baseball cap.

"Not Yankees fans, huh?" Harold said, sneering at Candice who remained silent, her head bowed.

Turning back to the two young guys approaching the Mercedes, Harold shouted, "Which one of you is the owner?"

"Yo, what's up?" the guy wearing the Yankees cap asked.

"What's up? What's up is you're either blind or you can't read," Harold said, pointing at the No Parking/No Stopping sign.

The guy made a dismissive gesture at the nearest sign. "We wuz just takin' a two second time-out to click some shots," he said, holding up a digital camera.

"Two seconds? We've been waiting for five minutes."

"Harold, please," Candice said, placing her hand on his thigh. "People are starting to stare."

"Not now," Harold growled, shaking her hand off his leg.

"What's your rush, anyway, old man?" the Yankees cap guy was now saying, starting to open the passenger side door. "Looks to me like you've got some good seats," he said, motioning to the carriage. "Why don't you just chill out with your lady and enjoy the scenery?"

"Don't tell me to chill out, you little pissant. And I'm still plenty young enough to kick your scrawny little ass. Now, move that hunk of shit!"

"Screw you, old man."

"Screw me, huh? I'll show you who's going to get screwed, you little pissant," Harold said, leaping out of the carriage and running towards the Mercedes.

All three boys were in the car before Harold's feet hit the asphalt. All three of them laughed and gave Harold the finger as the Mercedes peeled away from the curb.

"I'm gonna shove those fingers right up your asses!" Harold shouted after them.

"Yeah? Fuck you, old man!" the guy wearing the Yankees cap shouted back, turning completely around in the passenger seat and giving Harold the finger with both hands.

. . . . To Be Continued . . .

embarrassing?

"We should turn around and kick his ass," Jamaal said, continuing to give the old man the finger for another few seconds before turning around and plopping back down into the front passenger seat.

"Are you kidding?" Junior replied from the back seat. "Did you see that guy? He was huge."

"Whatever. He was old. And there's three of us. We woulda killed him."

"He was psychotic."

"You sayin' you was scared, Junior?"

"No. I'm saying we can't afford to get into trouble. Especially in another country."

Jamaal laughed. "This ain't Cambodia or Pakistan. It's Canada."

"So? They'd still throw us in jail."

"Yeah, like I'm so scared of Canadian jails. They probably give people manicures and pedicures in their jails."

Junior glared at the back of Jamaal's head. Ever since they crossed the border into Canada yesterday afternoon, he'd been regretting his decision to accompany Jamaal and Jamaal's best friend, Will, on their first annual Niagara Falls poker run. It was actually Will who had talked him into it, insisting the three of them could make a ton of money, telling him the Canadian side of the Falls was a Mecca for making money off rich rookie poker players. Of course, it wasn't until last night that Junior found out Jamaal and Will had already been on a first annual Atlantic City poker run two months ago and got cleaned out. Naturally, both Will and Jamaal provided a lengthy list of excuses for their downfall in Atlantic City and were confident that their luck would change once they'd crossed the border into Canada.

"Well, even if their jails are soft," Junior replied. "I can't afford to have a record in any country. I won't be able to get bonded and work in a bank or —"

"Relax, Junior. We're not going back," said Will, making a left onto Clifton Hill. "Besides," he added a moment later while surveying a group of young women cloistered in front of the War Memorial waiting for the arrival of the next tour bus. "We're going to get some eats."

"Now you're talking," Jamaal said. "We gotta make sure we got enough fuel for a long night of rounders. Where you wanna go?"

"How about the Rainforest Café?" Junior suggested.

Jamaal sniggered. "Sounds like a place for kiddies."

"It's not. It's really cool, actually. It's like this indoor tropical island with all kinds of animals jumping out at you and —"

"Would you check out Mr. Travel Brochure," Jamaal said, slapping Will and nodding in Junior's direction.

"Hey, I'm just sick of eating at Burger King or McDonalds," Junior said.

"And just what the hell is wrong with BK or Mickey-Dees?"

"Maybe if you'd watched *Supersize Me* like I told you to, you'd know."

"Whatever, man. I hate those stupid documentary movies. I'm keeping it real with the action and drama."

"Yeah, keeping it *real stupid*."

"Hey, you know something, Junior? I got a good mind to get Will here to circle back around and drop you off in Mr. Horse Carriage's lap so he can whoop your ass and get you thrown into jail."

"Would both of you chill out? Look at all this action you're missing," Will said, now pointing at a young woman with curly blonde hair wearing an aquamarine bikini top, matching volleyball shorts, and flip-flops sauntering along the sidewalk in front of Burger King.

"Ah, shit, man. You're right. What the hell am I doing wasting my breath on Junior here? I should be giving the ladies my undivided attention."

For the next few seconds all three boys scanned the cast of characters crowding the sidewalks along Clifton Hill, a cornucopia of canoodling couples and swinging singles, voyeurs and virgins, addicts and alcoholics, honeymooners and hookers, tourists and townies, first-time winners and lifetime losers, all backdropped by blazing neon and blaring billboards.

"Man, this is some crazy shit," Jamaal said, cruising a trio of transvestites gesturing at a couple of tourists holding several tiny tote bags.

"You want crazy? Check that out," Will said, easing the Mercedes to a halt behind a white pick-up truck stopped at the lights on the top of Clifton Hill.

"Where?"

"On the patio of that restaurant over there," Will replied, hoisting his thumb in the direction of Kelsey's restaurant. "Two *fine, fine* looking women."

Jamaal whistled when he saw them. "Well, well, well," he said, to Will, smiling. "Aren't they just about the sweetest lookin' honeys we seen all day. Sit tight, my pretty young things, 'cause we's about to bring the party to your house."

"I thought we were gonna check out the Rainforest Café?" Junior said.

Jamaal shook his head. "No. That was just your lame ass suggestion, which, thanks to those two lovely ladies, has just been vetoed."

"But I —"

"Hey," Jamaal snapped, turning around and shoving his index finger in Junior's face. "The only butts I'm interested in right now are the ones sittin' on that patio. Got it? Besides, there's only two of them. Which leaves you odd man out, anyway."

"Whatever."

"None of us is going anywhere until we find a parking spot," Will said, motioning to the near-gridlock traffic.

"Good luck," Junior replied. "This place is a zoo. It's totally —"

"Honk the horn, Will," Jamaal said, his gaze once again fixed on the two women on the patio.

"What? Why?"

"I wanna get the ladies' attention."

"Don't do it, Will," Junior said.

"What?" Jamaal snapped. "Why the fuck not?"

"Because it's embarrassing."

"Embarrassing?"

"Yeah. Will's gonna honk his horn. Everyone's gonna look. And then you're gonna shout out some crude remark and we're gonna look like world-class idiots."

"Will, honk the fuckin' horn before the light changes. I'm gonna show Junior here some fuckin' world-class class."

Will honked the horn, twice, causing nearly everyone seated in both the semi-enclosed and open-air patios of Kelsey's restaurant, as well as those persons walking along the sidewalks, to turn their heads in unison.

"Yo, ladies. Yeah, you two, right there," Jamaal shouted, pointing at the two women. "You ladies are the reason cavemen drew on walls!"

"And you're the reason women think most men are Neanderthals."

. . . . **To Be Continued . . .**

we're American

"Why'd you say that?" Tony asked, looking at his wife Gail with mild curiosity.

In the moments preceding Gail's comment, Tony had been browsing the restaurant's decor, taking in the framed photographs of various celebrities, as well as the collection of musical instruments and sporting memorabilia attached to the walls. His eyes had just fallen on a pair of antiquated tennis racquets when he'd heard the young guy in the black Mercedes convertible shouting at the two women seated at a nearby table followed, a moment later, by his wife's acerbic response.

"I said it because it was a cheesy line," Gail replied, momentarily regarding Tony as though he were a colossal idiot. "And he ripped it off Greg Kinnear's character in *As Good As It Gets*," she added, tearing off a large chunk of garlic bread.

Tony sighed as he watched the bread quickly disappear inside Gail's sizeable mouth, debating whether or not to suggest the real reason she didn't like what the guy in the convertible had said was because she wasn't the type of woman who caused men to honk their horns, let alone the type of woman who could cause someone to tell her she was the reason cavemen drew on walls.

"I don't know," Tony said, reaching for his glass of ginger ale. "I thought it was kind of romantic."

"Romantic?" Gail snorted, momentarily delaying her assault on a honey garlic chicken wing. "Pathetic, is more like it. If you're going to shout something that hundreds of people will overhear, at least have the courtesy of being original."

No, if anything, Gail was the type of woman that caused most men to fall to their knees in supplication to whatever higher being they believed in and pray that they never ended up with such a woman.

"That was nothing more than another example of life plagiarising art," Gail continued after chasing a mouthful of wing with a swig of beer. "How can he expect anyone to even appreciate let alone fall for a line someone used in a movie?"

In fact, Tony himself had made such a prayer on dozens of occasions. Possibly hundreds. Ever since he could remember, he wondered what his father had seen in his mother, wondered why he married such a boorish, opinionated, belligerent woman — and promised to not make the same mistake his father had concerning matters of the heart.

"Are you going to finish that?" Gail asked, deftly removing the last chicken wing from Tony's plate before he could reply.

Despite his prayers and promises, however, he *had* made the same mistake which, initially, caused him considerable confusion. His older brother had laughed and told Tony not to worry about it, that he was predestined to make the mistake, that some psychologist somewhere along the line figured out that sons were inclined to marry women who resembled their mothers in the same way that daughters were inclined to marry men who resembled their fathers. This would have made perfect sense and perhaps even eased Tony's confusion if it weren't for the fact that his brother was married to a very petite, very polite, and very conservative woman. When Tony pointed out this fact to his brother, his brother merely shrugged his shoulders and said that another psychologist figured out that, in some cases, children overcompensate by selecting partners who are the exact opposite of their parents.

"Can I take your plate for you, sir?"

A waitress, standing beside their booth, was pointing at Tony's empty dinner plate.

"Yes, of course," Tony replied, leaning back to allow the waitress to take his plate. "Thank you."

"And how was everything, sir?" the waitress asked.

"Great," Tony said, smiling graciously. "Everything was great."

"He's lying," Gail said, sucking on a chicken wing.

Unfortunately, Tony could not put the mistake down to being ignorant of Gail's natural disposition. Nor could he claim, as other men could, that his wife had changed once they'd been married since Gail was every bit as brash and outspoken when he first met her as she was now.

"Honey," Tony said, gently nudging her with his foot under the table.

"Stop kicking me," Gail snapped, pulling the chicken wing out of her mouth. Then, after inspecting it for any remnants of meat, she added, "He thought the garlic bread was too crispy and that you were trying to rip him off by putting too much ice in his ginger ale."

"I did *not* say that," Tony said, looking at the waitress and shaking his head in an attempt to reassure her that these words never left his mouth.

"Yes, but you were thinking it, weren't you?" Gail said.

"No, I was —"

"Are you calling me a liar?" Gail interrupted, looking up from her wing.

"No, I . . . was not calling you a, oh, never mind," Tony said, sighing. Then, turning to the waitress. "Okay, the truth is I did think the garlic bread was too crispy and that there was too much ice in my ginger ale."

"Well, sir, if you like, I can bring you another order of garlic bread and a ginger ale without ice."

Tony shook his head. "That's okay. I'm fine."

"You sure? It's no problem."

"No, really. I'm fine. Thanks," Tony said, taking a quick sip of his ginger ale to persuade her.

Smiling at Tony's sip of faith, the waitress turned to Gail. "And how about you, ma'am?"

"I'll have another draft if you promise never to call me ma'am again. Do we have a deal?"

104

The waitress laughed. "We do."

"Great. Bring on the draft, then."

It was precisely during these moments when Tony had an inkling as to why he proposed to Gail, when he knew why his father had married his mother: it was because other women, women such as his brother's wife, were boring by comparison. Gail was raw, unedited, and unrestrained. She ate the way she wanted, dressed the way she wanted, said what she wanted, and, as much as Tony could tell, appeared to live unhindered by the usual societal norms governing a woman's conduct.

As the waitress walked out of earshot, Tony considered asking Gail why she felt compelled to tell the waitress he was lying. Of course, he didn't. He already knew Gail would respond by telling him that his life would be considerably more productive and a lot less stressful if he didn't spend all his time keeping things inside, thinking he should've said this or that, creating a variety of scenarios in his mind of the way things could have been if only he'd opened his mouth.

Instead, for the moment, he returned his gaze to the old tennis racquets. They reminded him of the ones he and his sister used when they played at the courts outside their high school in Manitoba and it was just as he recalled the time his sister beat him for the first time that his attention and gaze, once again, drifted to a nearby couple. In what Tony guessed was their early forties, attractive, thin, and stylishly dressed, they looked like the sort of couple you'd see splashed on the cover of an L.L. Bean or Eddie Bauer catalogue. He'd been watching them since they'd sat down a few minutes after he and Gail arrived, surprised by the quantity of food they'd initially ordered — two appetizers and two main courses each. He was fully expecting another couple or perhaps their teenage children to join them, then watched in amazement as they devoured all four appetizers and main courses before ordering and easily finishing two desserts each, the entire time wondering how they managed to stay so thin.

"Would you listen to that chick?"

Tony returned his gaze to Gail. "Which one?"

"Which one? Are you kidding? Listen."

A moment later, Tony heard someone singing harmony to the Celine Dion song coming through the restaurant's speaker system. Turning his head in the direction of the voice, Tony saw it was one of the young women the men in the black Mercedes had shouted at. A shoo-in for a younger, prettier Whitney Houston, the woman was bent slightly forward, her eyes closed, her mouth hovering inches over the long, slender glass of her strawberry daiquiri, as though she were using it as a microphone.

"I thought you liked that song?"

"I do. When Celine sings it. Unaccompanied."

Tony smiled. "I'm impressed that someone her age actually knows the words. It's more than a few years removed from her generation."

"I don't care if she knows the words. She sounds horrible," Gail said, abruptly twirling around in her seat and shouting, "Hey, Miss Singalong!"

The young woman stopped singing immediately and opened her eyes. "Me?" she asked, pointing at herself.

"Yeah, you," Gail replied. "Do you see a sign anywhere saying, 'Canadian Idol auditions'?"

"We're American," the young woman replied, snottily.

"Good for you, honey. But I don't see any signs saying 'American Idol auditions' either, do you?"

When the young woman didn't respond after a few seconds, deciding, instead, to exchange 'Who the hell is this lady?' glances with her dinner companion, Gail snorted.

"I didn't think so," she said. "Now, seeing as there aren't any audition signs around here and this isn't a karaoke bar, why don't we just let the real artists sing their songs without you butchering them? Can we do that?"

. . . . **To Be Continued . . .**

fashion is a tough business

"What a monumental bitch," Tania said under her breath.

"Ignore her. She's obviously deranged," Kulsum replied, giving the woman a dirty look but secretly applauding her for saying what she'd said.

Ever since Tania won a singing contest in high school five years ago and someone at her modelling class said she looked like a young Whitney Houston, Tania felt it necessary to sing along to every song she heard, especially when she and Kulsum were in public.

"You're right," Tania replied. "What were we talking about?"

"When?"

"Before."

"Before when?"

"I don't know, the last thing we were talking about."

"I can't rememb—"

"Fashion!" Tania nearly shouted after her eyes fell on the framed photograph of Marilyn Monroe. "That was it. So, I think we should do it."

"Do what?"

"Start our own clothing line."

"I don't know," Kulsum said, trying to sound as disinterested as possible, allowing her gaze to wander aimlessly along the row of petunia-filled baskets hanging on the cast iron railing beside her. "It's a pretty big risk."

The truth was Kulsum had no desire to go into business with Tania. Even though she acknowledged that Tania was intelligent and probably had an above average business acumen — especially for someone her age — this did not excuse the fact, at least in Kulsum's mind, that Tania was also annoying, conceited, and always had to get her way.

A simple example of this was dinner. Kulsum had wanted to go to a less touristy restaurant, something with a little more local colour, but Tania had pulled another one of her infamous hissy fits, telling Kulsum she wanted to sit on a patio — with a view. The view she was referring to, of course, was of herself. She always wanted to be within reach of as many eyes as possible, and patios provided much more exposure than fully enclosed restaurants.

Unfortunately for Tania, her first choice — Kelsey's open-air patio located on arguably the busiest corner in Niagara Falls — was full and had a waiting list. Reluctantly, she settled for her second choice — a street-side table on Kelsey's semi-enclosed patio overlooking most of Clifton Hill. After being seated and briefed on the specials of the day, Tania began employing a variety of "attention-seeking" techniques including — but not confined to — primping her hair, angling her cleavage, using unnecessarily flamboyant hand gestures, batting her eyes, and singing. In the past, Kulsum had known Tania to become increasingly distraught when she didn't receive her RDA of attention within an allotted time from those persons within eyesight of her. This often inspired increasingly flagrant attempts to get it. Fortunately, thanks to their waiter (who had already come by their table at least a dozen times to flirt with her and give them free drinks), the man sitting across from them who couldn't keep his eyes off her, and the three guys in the black Mercedes, Tania's need to be noticed had been adequately addressed.

"It's not that big a risk," Tania was now saying.

"Sure it is," Kulsum said, her gaze now continuing past the petunia baskets to the large neon "Frankenstein" sign across the street. "Fashion is a tough business. It's always changing."

"I know fashion is a tough business. I used to be a model. I know how —"

"You went to modelling *classes*," Kulsum corrected.

"I modelled."

"You never got paid for it."

"So?"

"Well, it's not modelling if you don't get paid for it."

"Anyway, that's not even the point. The point is I know fashion is always changing. But that's precisely how all the great fashion designers make their money. They convince people that things are out of style as soon as they buy them. I mean, the big design companies do it all the time. Gap, Liz Claiborne, Tommy Hilfiger — all of them design clothes that have a built-in expiration date. Do you realise they have fashion shows in Europe and the UK right now that are three seasons ahead? That means the 'Best Before' date on the clothes and styles we're wearing right now expired almost a year ago. So, what do you think?"

"I think you're crazy!"

. . . . **To Be Continued . . .**

you want to go first?

"Sorry," Shelley said, to the two young women seated in the booth across from her and Jim and, when the two women went back to their conversation, she frowned at Jim and said, "Could you please keep your voice below one hundred decibels?"

"Sure, if you can refrain from making ludicrous statements."

"What was so ludicrous?"

"Saying you admire Jeffrey Dahmer. The guy was a sick, psychopathic, serial killer."

"True. But he was also a firm believer in *mea culpa*."

"And *that's* why you admire him?"

Shelley nodded. "Look around you, we're a bunch of blamers. We don't accept responsibility for anything we do anymore."

Jim was about to reply to Shelley's statement when the waitress arrived and handed him his change.

"Thanks," he said, putting the coins in his pocket and leaving the twenty dollar bill on the table.

"That's the tip?" Shelley asked.

Jim nodded. "Not enough?"

"I was thinking it was too much."

Jim shrugged. "I really enjoyed the meal. Didn't you?"

"Yeah, it was great. But that's a twenty-five per cent tip."

"It's okay. She deserved it. It was great service. Bathroom?"

"Of course. Men's or Ladies'?"

"We went to the Ladies' for lunch."

"Men's it is, then. After you, sir."

"Thanks," Jim said, getting up and starting to walk in the direction of the washrooms. "So, you were saying something about us being a society of blamers?"

Shelley nodded. "It's true. I mean, nowadays, whenever you try to get someone to accept responsibility for something they did, their fingers start pointing in a million different directions. They blame their parents or society or their brother as their rationale for why they decided to blow up a daycare centre or steal a car or become an alcoholic. It's so rare to hear someone say, 'It's my fault. I'm to blame.'"

"And Dahmer did?" Jim asked, reaching the door to the Men's bathroom.

"As a matter of fact, yes, he did."

Jim ducked his head into the washroom and, after seeing it was empty, gestured for Shelley to follow him. "And when did he do this?"

"At his trial."

"Really?"

"Yep."

Walking into the first stall, Jim lifted the toilet seat. "You want to go first?"

"Sure," Shelley replied, following him into the stall and closing the door. "Can you hold my hair back?"

"Of course."

After moving into position, Shelley bent over the toilet, waiting for Jim to gather up all her hair before sticking her finger down her throat and vomiting her partially digested apple strudel, molten lava cake, shrimp pasta Alfredo, balsamic chicken penne, chicken wings, and garden salad into the toilet water.

"You okay?" Jim asked when she stopped heaving.

Shelley nodded. "Fine," she said, slightly out of breath and spitting in the toilet.

"Done?"

She spat again, then raised her head. "Done."

"Here," Jim said, still holding her hair and handing her a small handkerchief.

113

"Thanks," she said, wiping her mouth.

"My turn," Jim said. They switched positions and Jim stuck his finger in his mouth, shoving it further and further back until he felt his stomach violently lurch, quickly pulling out his finger as the food raced past his esophageal sphincter, shot out of his mouth, and splashed into the toilet bowl, his New York–style cheesecake, apple strudel, Mediterranean vegetable and chicken fusilli, English-style fish and chips, Greek salad, and chicken wings mixing with Shelley's regurgitated meal.

"Okay?" Shelley asked.

"Fine," Jim replied, standing up and taking the handkerchief from Shelley and wiping his mouth.

"How do I look?" Shelley asked, smiling, showing her teeth.

"All clear," Jim replied. "Me?"

"You've got a little something on your cheek," she said, picking it off and examining it. "It looks like a bacon bit," she said before flicking it into the toilet and flushing it.

"Thanks."

"No problem," she replied, popping a piece of gum into her mouth and taking a few chews before giving Jim a long, deep, soulful kiss, leaving the piece of gum in his mouth.

"Mmmm," he said, as they exited the stall. "Cinnamon. My favourite."

"Mine too."

"Good job."

"Couldn't have done it without you."

"I love you."

"I love you, too."

They kissed again.

"Shall we?" Jim said, motioning to the washroom door.

"After you, my love," Shelley replied.

Jim opened the washroom door, took a peek, then motioned for her to follow. "So, Dahmer said it was his fault, huh?"

Shelley nodded. "At his trial he made a point of saying it was his

fault, that he accepted full responsibility," she said, pulling out an article from her faux-leather purse. "In fact, I have the evidence right here.
Dahmer told the court, and I quote, 'As far as I'm concerned, they're
all excuses. I feel it's wrong for people to try and shift the blame onto
somebody else, onto their parents or onto their upbringing or living
circumstances. I think that's just a cop-out. I take full responsibility.'"

"Impressive," Jim said, nodding his head with approval. "But, then
again, it's not like he shouldn't have taken responsibility. He committed a pretty heinous crime."

"I agree," Shelley said, putting the article back in her purse. "And
I'm not arguing that. I'm just admiring the fact that he was able to
admit it. He didn't run away from his responsibility. He understood
his actions had consequences and was prepared to —"

"Did you honestly think you were going to get away with it, you
stupid little pissant?"

Shelley and Jim turned in the direction of the voice and saw a man,
probably in his fifties, his face crimson, the veins on his thick neck
bulging, squaring off with a young black guy wearing a New York
Yankees baseball cap.

"Harold! Don't!" shouted a woman standing near the man,
presumably the man's wife.

"You want some of this, old man?" said the young guy in the Yankees
cap. "You want some of this, huh? Well here it comes, muther —"

At this point the young guy stopped speaking because the older
man's fist was already in his mouth. A split second later, Shelley heard
a sickening crack, saw the young guy's baseball cap fly off his head,
saw him staggering backwards, his eyes rolling in their sockets
moments before his entire body crumpled, collapsing on the sidewalk
as though he was a marionette who'd just had his strings cut.

The older man took a few steps towards the young guy, momentarily hovering over the prostrate body with his mouth wide open,
screaming defiantly at the young guy before kicking the Yankees cap
and spinning around, a maniacal expression on his face, searching the
crowd like a caged wolverine expecting another attack.

Two young guys ran at him.

"You're dead, old man!" one of them shouted.

"We're gonna fuck you up," the other said.

Days later, in conversation with friends back in their hometown of Halifax, Jim and Shelley would tell them that it wasn't a controlled or calculated fight, like the kind you see on TV where two top-ranked boxers stalk each other, occasionally unleashing a flurry of punches — a well-disciplined combination of attacks and counterattacks, until one of them connects hard enough or often enough to render his opponent unconscious or unable to continue.

"This," Jim would tell them, "was an out-of-control brawl. There were arms and legs flailing every which way. Wild swings and misses. Pushing, shoving, grabbing. Even so, it was obvious, right from the start, that the two younger guys didn't stand a chance. Sure the man was older, but he was incredibly strong. He had that kind of strength you only get from doing a lot of physical labour. And rage. He had so much rage in him. It was as though he was saving it up for these three guys. Like he had a ton of issues he needed to work through and taking it out on them was his substitute for therapy or something. It was awesome."

"It wasn't awesome," Shelley would say. "It was *awful*. You should have seen what those three guys looked like afterwards."

"Is that when you think you were pickpocketed?" one of their friends would ask.

Jim would nod. "Guaranteed. Thinking back on it now, I'm not so sure they didn't stage the whole thing."

"Really?"

Shelley would disagree with Jim on this point. "I don't think so," she would say. "There's no way you could fake that fight. All that blood. And those cracking sounds. You can't fake a head smacking off the sidewalk or ribs breaking."

"What did he do after he beat up the other two guys?"

"He just stood there, yelling at them."

116

"What was he saying?"

"Now who's laughing? Now who's giving who the finger, huh?" the man screamed, giving the three grounded and bleeding bodies the finger with both hands.

There was no response from the three guys, only moans and, in the case of the guy with the Yankees cap, silence.

"Harold! Please! Let's go."

"What's the rush? I didn't do nothing wrong. It was self-defence. Everyone here saw it. These three pissants started the whole thing."

"Harold. Please."

"Okay, okay. I'm coming. I need a drink," the man said, heading in the direction of Kelsey's.

"We can't go in there now!" the woman said, pulling frantically on his arm, causing the man to careen into Shelley, who, in turn, bumped into a fellow spectator, a thin boy carrying a satchel.

"Sorry," Shelley said to the boy.

"No worries," the boy replied, quickly tucking Shelley's wallet into his satchel before catching sight of his father, who was now motioning for the boy to follow him.

. . . . To Be Continued . . .

loser buys . . . .

Walter waited until he and his son Billy were walking past two street vendors displaying their wares along Victoria Street before he spoke.

"How'd you make out, son?"

"I got three."

"Not bad."

"You?"

"Two."

"*Only* two?"

Walter smiled in response to the mixture of surprise and excitement in his son's voice.

"You only lifted two, Dad?"

Walter nodded. "You have to make allowances. I was admiring my boy's handiwork. The lift on the woman's purse was spectacular. Textbook. I couldn't have done it better myself."

"Thanks, Dad," Billy replied, beaming.

"No problem. Now, let's go see what we got," Walter said, motioning towards the bench beneath the nearby overhang.

Walter was a fifth-generation pickpocket. His father, reputed to be one of the best pickpockets in North America, had tried to lift JFK's wallet when the then President Elect came to Niagara Falls in 1960. Unfortunately, he only got close enough to lift the wallet of a Secret Service agent, which he proudly displayed in a large, bulletproof, glass cabinet in his den. He'd also had his hand in the drug trade, as well as a finger or two in almost anything else that required covert access across the Canada–U.S. border.

Walter began his apprenticeship with his father when he was eight. By the time he was thirteen, he was making more money in a year than most men three times his age made working legitimate jobs. His favourite marks were Americans. He figured that since the Americans had been screwing Canadians over for years with the exchange rate on the dollar, it was his civic duty as a good Canadian to get some of it back. By the time his own son, Billy, was ten, they were working as a team during weekends and summer holidays, cruising up and down Clifton Hill, hanging around the souvenir shops, amusement parks, and restaurants like Burger King and Kelsey's that were normally packed with tourists.

"You first, son," Walter said to Billy as they sat down on one of the benches. "Who do you have?"

"A Mr. Jim Dyer. And a Mrs. Shelley Dyer."

"From?"

"Nova Scotia. Halifax."

"It's too bad they weren't American."

"I thought they were."

"Me, too," Walter said, sensing the disappointment in his son's voice. "But, hey, it's not too often you get a husband-and-wife combo. They'll have a couple of nice memories to take back home with them to Halifax: a world class brawl and their wallets stolen — all on the same night. How much did they give you?"

"Two hundred and ten, plus a MasterCard."

"Very nice. Next?"

"One Mr. Derek Apple from Eugene, Oregon, with a Visa Gold card and what looks to be, let's see — one, two, three, four, five, six, seven — one hundred and forty American."

"Nice. After converting the American money that'll leave you with just over four hundred bucks. Not bad for a couple minutes work, son. Not bad at all."

"Thanks, Dad. What did you end up with?"

"Well, I have a Mr. Jeremy White from Hagersville, Ontario, with an American Express card and a Visa Platinum card but only twenty bucks U.S. to his name. And a Mr. Shaun Milligan from Hamilton, Ontario, with, well, lookee here, it's Mr. Big Ticket. One hundred. One fifty. Two hundred. Two twenty, forty — two hundred and fifty bucks Canadian. Thank you, Shaun."

"Looks like you're still buying dinner, though, Dad."

"What do you mean?"

Billy gestured to his loot. "I pulled in over four hundred, almost half of it American. You only got just shy of three hundred, all of it Canadian. Loser buys. Your rules, Dad."

"Who said anything about losing?" Walter said, pulling out his cell phone and dialling a number. "Yeah, Joey. I got one . . . A Mercedes convertible . . . Black. Looks like it just rolled off the assembly line today . . . Yeah, I'm looking at it right now . . . American plates. New York State . . . I've got the keys in my hands . . . Sure, how long? . . . Ten minutes suits me just fine. Make sure you bring the cash . . . Nice try. Three large or I call Roy . . . Hey, I was doing you a favour calling you first. You want me to call Roy? . . . You sure? . . . Yep, the usual spot . . . That's right. Okay, I'll see you in ten."

"Whose keys are those?" Billy asked when his father hung up his cell phone.

"One of the kids that got his ass whooped."

"When did you lift them?"

"Just before his buddy got his face smashed in by the old guy."

"You're incredible, Dad."

"Thank you. And, with the three thousand bucks I'm gonna get from Roy for an *American*-owned car, that brings my total up to just shy of thirty-three hundred bucks. So, it looks like you're the one buying dinner again, son."

"Damn," Billy said.

Walter gave Billy's leg a whack. "Don't cuss, son."

"Sorry, Dad. I just don't understand why I have to buy you dinner when you made almost ten times as much as I did."

"It's the way of the world, son. It's how the rich get richer."

Billy sighed. "Well, where would you like to go?"

Walter took a moment to consider his options. "My first inclination is to hit the buffet at the casino again. But, upon further review, I'm thinking maybe we should try some place a little classier. The Sundowner sound good to you?"

Billy smiled. "I don't think I'm old enough, Dad."

"Soon enough, my boy. Soon enough," Walter said, reaching over and ruffling his son's hair. Then, catching sight of a familiar face walking across the street, he said, "Speaking of the Sundowner, I think that's what's-her-name over there."

"Where?"

"In front of Howard Johnson's," Walter replied, pointing across the street, his eyes focussing on the woman wearing a bouquet of blonde curls, an aquamarine bikini top, matching volleyball shorts, and flip-flops standing outside the hotel. "Yep, that's her, alright," Walter said, after a moment.

"Who is she, Dad?"

"Candi!" Walter shouted, beginning to wave. "Hey, Candi! Over here!"

. . . . **To Be Continued . . .**

cat calls　.　.　.　.　.　.　.　.　.　.　.　.　.　.　.　.　.　.

Nadine immediately began walking in the direction of Clifton Hill in
an effort to put some distance between her and the guy shouting her
stage name.

It wasn't the first time Nadine had been recognised outside of
work. Last fall, when she was performing in Montreal, one of her
professors had asked her for a lap dance, not realising it was her until
she politely declined his invitation, telling him that it might be
construed as a conflict of interest.

She got the idea of being an entertainer from her older sister, Silvia.
Silvia had graduated from university with a degree in Biology, then
tried for two years to find a job in her field before deciding to return
to university to get her Masters degree. Two years later, armed with two
degrees, she still wasn't able to find a decent paying job. At twenty-
eight, Silvia was now living at home with their parents in Ottawa,
working as a part-time instructor at Carleton University, and barely
making the minimum payments on her outstanding student loans.

Since Nadine had no intention of following in her sister's foot-
steps, during her first year at university she worked as a waitress and
then, the day she turned nineteen, she celebrated by getting up on
stage at the Sundowner in Niagara Falls. That summer she became a
regular on the Montreal-Toronto-Hamilton–Niagara Falls entertainment circuit, making enough money to pay for that year's tuition,
books, food, and rent at university — as well as an almost new Pontiac
Sunfire and several new custom-designed outfits.

Last summer she'd met a woman online interested in launching a personal fulfilment service catering to an exclusive clientele. The two of them agreed to meet in Toronto, had each liked what the other had to offer, and immediately formed a partnership. Two weeks after creating a Web site detailing their services, they performed their first show in the penthouse suite at Casino Niagara for a group of women from San Francisco, leaving the hotel two hours later with $1500 each. This was a typical evening's pay. Their rates ran anywhere from $1000 for an hour of relatively standard fun to $8000 for an entire evening of *extreme* entertainment, the type of entertainment your wife, husband, or significant other would neither permit nor perform.

It was, in fact, her partner who Nadine was waiting to hear back from as she continued down Victoria Street, striding quickly past the Asian man encouraging her to buy a rice necklace with her name on it; past the vendor selling sketches of Eminem, Bob Marley, Jackie Chan, JFK, and Jessica Simpson; past The Loveboat restaurant and a souvenir store; past the woman snapping her fingers in front of her husband's face to distract his gaze from Nadine's breasts; past the convenience store advertising "authentic Cuban cigars"; waving in mid-stride at Troy and Jess who were at their usual spot, seated on the rocks across the street, hawking their beaded trinkets, hemp necklaces, and hash pipes; noticing an unusually large crowd of people gathered outside Kelsey's; ignoring the horn honks and cat calls from a group of teenage boys packed into a souped-up Volkswagen Golf that temporarily drowned out the sound of approaching sirens; before eventually ducking into Sauer's Drug Store and purchasing a package of chewing gum.

A few minutes later, stepping out of the drugstore, Nadine noticed the large crowd outside Kelsey's had been joined by two ambulances and several police cruisers. Drawing nearer, she saw three young men being put into the ambulances, one of them on a stretcher. An older man, in handcuffs, was being escorted by two officers into the back of a cruiser while a woman, presumably his wife, screamed hysterically.

Nadine had just decided to cross the street to get a better look when her cell phone rang. She reached into her purse, flipped open her phone and saw her partner's stage name on her call display screen. Smiling, she put the phone to her ear and said hello.

. . . . **To Be Continued . . .**

not tonight, darling . . . .

"Darling, how are you? . . . Good . . . Me? Oh, fabulous, as usual. Where
are you? . . . Of course you are . . . Because you love it there. Personally,
I think it's a dreadful place. All those tacky tourist traps. So, tell me,
darling, how have you been spending your time, parading up and down
the strip in a pair of flip-flops and a bikini top? . . . Just as I suspected.
If only our clients knew you were so bourgeois . . . Yes. They called to
confirm this afternoon . . . Hmmm? . . . Four women. From Italy.
They've rented a suite at the Royal York . . . I was thinking the same
thing: it has been a while since we had Italian . . . Of course, darling.
You know me. Finances first. Everything is in order. They'll be expecting us at midnight . . . Hmmm? . . . Certainly. Shall we say in the lobby,
fifteen minutes prior? . . . Excellent. I'll see you then. *Ciao*, darling."

"Who was that?"

Barbara had spent the late afternoon and early evening lounging
beside the pool, alternately reading back issues of *Toronto Life* and flipping through summer fashion magazines while nibbling hors
d'oeuvres and keeping her Singapore Sling topped up.

Moments before she'd heard Nixon, her husband, ask who was on
the phone, she'd been thinking how perfect things were — the warm
breeze, her cool drink, the slowly setting sun beginning to streak the
otherwise postcard-blue sky with generous slices of lavender and
ochre, the news about the Italian women, the fact that Nixon wasn't
sitting beside her, boring her with talk of investing more of her money
in some unscrupulous scheme of his.

"Just a friend," Barbara replied, slowly setting the portable phone
down on the patio table next to her chaise lounge.

"What's his name?"

Barbara smirked, then pulled her sunglasses down over her eyes.

"There's hardly enough sun to merit sunglasses, you know."

"It's not the sun I'm trying to block out, darling."

Nixon growled. "I'm sick of this."

"Of what, darling?"

"Of your secrets."

Barbara smiled. "I thought you preferred them."

"To what?"

"To the truth."

"I never said that."

"Not in so many words," Barbara said, taking a sip of her drink. "I merely thought we had an understanding."

"An understanding?"

"Yes. The understanding that I have my secrets, you have yours, we both know they exist but we don't trouble ourselves about them."

"Well, I'm tired of it."

Barbara chuckled. "Don't tell me you'd rather we started being honest with each other?"

Nixon hesitated a moment. "That's precisely what I'm saying."

Barbara set her drink down on the table next to her and pushed her sunglasses onto the top of her head. "You can't be serious?"

"Well, I am."

"Did you stop off at Vinny's again before you got home?" she asked, pointing to his whiskey tumbler.

"I'm not drunk, if that's what you're insinuating."

"You're quite sure?"

"Yes, quite."

"Too much sun then?"

"What are you getting at?"

"I'm merely curious as to what has inspired this sudden change."

"I just think it's time we cleared the air, don't you?"

Barbara reached down and grabbed the portable phone off the patio table.

"What are you doing?"

"I'm calling Patty Jenkins."

"Why?"

"To get the number of her shrink. You obviously need help."

"Screw you, Barbara."

"I'm serious. I've never seen you like this."

"Put the phone down, Barbara."

"As you wish, darling," Barbara said, sighing and putting down the phone. "No one can say I didn't try."

Nixon swallowed a mouthful of whiskey. "You know what I think?"

"Heavens, no. I stopped trying to figure out what you think years ago."

"I think you're afraid to tell the truth."

"On the contrary, darling. I am quite prepared to tell the truth. However, I fail to see how either of us will benefit from such an exchange."

"Well, it's a helluva lot better than slinking around making a mockery of our vows."

Barbara thought about this for a moment. "I'm not so sure I agree. After all, we've been doing this for almost twelve years now. Granted, it's not the ideal situation, but then again, who's to say?"

"Well, I'm tired of it. I want things to change."

Barbara took a quick sip of her drink. "Are you sure you wouldn't rather go to confession?"

"Will you stop patronising me?"

"I'm just trying to offer you alternatives, darling," Barbara said, getting up from her chaise lounge and starting to walk towards the outdoor bar fridge. "This may not be the best idea you've ever had, you know."

"Now where are you going?"

"Refill," she replied, pointing to her near-empty glass. "Plus I want to give you time to reconsider."

"I don't need time."

"Another drink then?"

"I'm fine," Nixon snapped.

"Suit yourself," she said, refilling her glass from the sizeable jug of Singapore Sling mix before returning to her chaise lounge. "Now what?"

"Now we start telling each other our dirty little secrets."

"Shall we toss a coin to see who goes first?"

"You can go first, if you like."

"It's your game. I think you should. After all, I really have no idea how dirty you want to get."

"Okay. I'll start," Nixon growled. "I married you for your money. I've never really loved you."

"Well, so much for starting slow."

"It's the truth."

"I'm not doubting it. If it's any consolation, I've never really loved you either, darling. I agreed to marry you because I'd just broken up with the one and only love of my life and was completely devastated. When I heard he'd left me for another woman and asked her to marry him, I wanted to beat him to the altar. And I did."

"I hate your hair colour."

"I don't colour my hair."

"I know. And I hate it. I also detest your skin."

"My skin? Why, for heaven's sake?"

"Because it's not normal. It should have aged at least a little by now."

"What can I say? I'm blessed with great tone."

"Well, it's not normal and I hate it."

"Would it make you happy if I went out and got wrinkle implants?"

"Very funny. Your turn."

"I was the one who keyed your car."

"What?"

Barbara nodded. "It was getting so tedious seeing you out there in the driveway every weekend washing it, parading around the thing like some middle-aged peacock, showing off for the neighbours."

"You fucking bitch."

"I don't know why you're so upset. I was the one who bought you the damn thing."

Nixon took a sip of his whiskey. "I may have slept around once or twice."

"To be expected, darling."

"You're not mad?"

Barbara shrugged. "I probably would be if I hadn't slept with our pool boy last summer."

"Ricardo?"

She nodded.

"My God, Barbara. The boy's not even old enough to vote."

"He will be. Next summer," Barbara said, smiling.

"You're, you're . . ."

"Yes?"

"I screwed our housekeeper."

"I know."

"Is that why you fired her?

"No, I fired her because she didn't clean the sheets afterwards."

"You're fucking incredible, you know that?"

"Thank you. Speaking of which, I *can* have children."

"What?"

"It's true. I'm perfectly healthy. There's nothing wrong with me."

"You mean you, you . . ."

"Faked the endometriosis? Yes."

"But how come you never, you know, got —"

"Pregnant? I've been on the pill the entire time."

Nixon tightened his grip on the whiskey tumbler until his arm began to shake. "You . . . you *cunt*! You cold-hearted, callous *cunt*!" he bellowed.

Barbara smiled. "Lovely game we're playing, don't you think, darling?"

"Who was that on the phone?"

"I told you, a friend."

"Who is he?"

"Not a he, a she. And, if you must know, she's a co-worker."

"A co-worker? How can you have a co-worker when you haven't

worked a day in your life?"

"True. And I suppose if I really think about it, this is more pleasure than work."

"What are you talking about?"

"My friend and I started our own personal fulfilment business a while ago."

"Personal what?"

"Fulfilment. We do this little mother-daughter routine. It's quite a big hit with our clientele, actually."

"A mother-daughter routine? How old is she?"

"Twenty-one."

"You mean to tell me you're pimping around with some dumb slut half your age?"

"Darling, please. I'm years away from being forty-two. And my friend is not a slut. And she's certainly not dumb. She's a year away from completing an undergraduate degree in organic chemistry. Do you have any idea how difficult organic chemistry is?"

"I don't give a rat's ass, Barbara. I'm more interested in knowing what you've got yourself mixed up in?"

"If you want to find out you can book an appointment. Mind you, it's fairly costly. I'm not so sure you'd be able to afford it, especially after calling me the c-word."

At that moment the phone rang.

"Don't answer that," Nixon snapped.

Ignoring him, Barbara picked up the phone and read the call display. "Perfect," she said, smiling. "It's Patty Jenkins. Something tells me you'll definitely need the number of her shrink now that we've aired our dirty little secrets."

"Fuck you, Barbara. Fuck. You."

"Not tonight, darling. I've got a show to do," Barbara replied. Then, hitting the SEND button on the phone, she brought it to her ear. "Patty, darling. How are you?"

. . . . To Be Continued . . .

she's going to be our first star . . . .

"Horrible. The kids are driving me crazy . . . No, this time it's Brett . . . Oh, I don't know. He's just so full of attitude. I can't even breathe right now I'm so angry with him . . . I know. I know. I was just wondering what you're doing . . . Oh, that sounds nice. So, are you busy? . . . No? You sure? . . . Well, would you mind if I come over for a while to cool down, maybe go for a dip in the pool? . . . Thanks. You're a lifesaver, Barbara. I'll be over in a few minutes."

Patty hung up the phone. "Thank God she was home," she said, letting out a long sigh of relief. "I don't know what I would've done."

Since Patty's psychologist, Robert Cairns, wasn't available on weekends — even by phone — she'd decided to call her semi-close and substantially wealthier friend, Barbara. A dip in the pool at Barbara's, along with a few cocktails, a joint, and some conversation should be enough to patch her through until she could make an appointment with the psychologist on Monday.

Rifling through her bathing suit drawer, Patty instinctively pulled out a bikini before reconsidering and opting for a one piece. She normally wore a bikini except when visiting Barbara who, at age thirty-nine, had the unblemished, no-stretch-marked, cellulite-free body of a twenty-two-year-old model. Just one of the innumerable advantages of not having three kids.

Patty hadn't wanted to have three kids. She'd only wanted one: a girl. When they had Brett, she and Barry tried again and ended up with twin boys. Barry said he was willing to try again if she wanted but Patty refused, insisting he get a vasectomy instead.

After pulling on a T-shirt and a pair of shorts over her bathing suit, Patty reached into her sock drawer and pulled out a bag of marijuana from inside a pair of slouch socks. Withdrawing two small joints from the Ziploc bag, she slipped them into her purse before stuffing the Ziploc bag back into her sock and closing the drawer.

"I'm going over to Barbara's," Patty announced as she walked downstairs into the living room.

"Be back soon?" Barry asked, looking up from his *Maclean's* magazine.

"I'll call you. Are you still going to that meeting?"

Barry nodded.

"Good luck. Hopefully you can find something we can use," Patty said, glaring at her son Brett.

He was seated on the living room floor, his back to her, his left ear plugged into his iPod, his eyes glued to the TV screen, playing hockey on PlayStation. She shook her head. If he and his brothers weren't watching TV, they were playing games on it. Hopeless, she said to herself. Bloody hopeless. "I want the bathroom spotless before you go anywhere tonight, Brett," she shouted, wanting to be sure he heard her above the music being pumped into his ear.

"I heard you the first three times," Brett groaned while shaking his head, his voice heavy with sarcasm.

Patty could feel the frustration fermenting in her stomach. In her mind she imagined walking over and cuffing Brett on the side of his head, smashing his stupid PlayStation and iPod and the goddamn TV to smithereens, and telling him that if he thought he had life so figured out then he should get the hell out of her house. "Life isn't always going to be this easy, mister. And the sooner you realise it the better!" she shouted before walking out the front door.

"Whatever," Brett sighed, continuing to play his game.

Waiting until he heard his wife's car door slam shut, Barry lowered the *Maclean's* magazine to his lap and pulled off his reading glasses. "You know, Brett, I've been meaning to ask you something for a while now."

"Shoot, Dad."

"What exactly does 'whatever' mean?"

Brett shrugged. "I don't know."

"And what does that mean?"

Brett rolled his eyes. "If you have to ask, Dad, you're too old to understand."

"Hey, I'm not that old."

"Dad, come on. You're ancient. You're a fossil."

Barry smiled. "I'm quite certain I don't predate the modern era."

"Whatever, Dad. They didn't even have CDs when you were growing up."

"True, there may not have been CDs or PCs or DVDs or MP3s or iPods or PlayStations or flat screen TVs or any of those things, but it wasn't that long ago that I was the one sitting on the floor, listening to my Walkman, playing Atari, and rolling my eyes at my dad when he was trying to talk to me."

Brett turned around and looked at his father like he was on drugs.

"It's true," Barry said. "Just because the technological gadgets have changed doesn't mean I didn't have the same thoughts as you're having. I still dreamed about being rich, driving a great car, finding a great gal. Or two. Travelling to places like France or Mexico or California. Maybe winning a lottery or being famous. But reality is usually something far different. Which is what your mother and I are trying to prepare you for."

"I am prepared."

Barry smiled. "That's exactly what I told my father."

Brett sighed. "So?"

Barry set aside his magazine and leaned forward in the sofa. "Listen, Brett, I'm not saying your mother and I have all the answers."

"You guys sure act like you do."

Barry smiled, doing his best not to react to the snotty tone of Brett's last comment. "I can see why you might think that's the case," he said after a few moments. "But did you ever stop to think why it seems we act that way?"

"Huh?"

"Let me put it this way: what is the one thing your mother and I have that you don't?"

"Rules?"

"Experience. And, whether you want to admit it or not, like Søren Kierkegaard said, 'Life is lived forward but understood backwards.'"

"Søren who?"

"Kierkegaard. He was a Swedish philosopher."

"So you're trying to say that I don't understand my life?"

"Not as well as you will twenty, heck, even five years from now."

"But it's *my* life. It's not yours."

"We realise it's your life, son."

"So then what's your point?"

"Actually I have two points. The first is that when I got to be about twenty-five or so, I realised my dad was right — I didn't have it all figured out. I wasn't prepared. And since he'd already been through a lot of the stuff I was going through or was about to go through, part of me wished I had trusted his experience. It would've saved me a lot of hassle."

"What's the second?"

"The second point is that we all change. Even you, son."

Brett smirked.

"Oh, you think you won't, huh?"

Brett shook his head. "Doubtful."

"Brett, my boy, in a few short years you'll look back on this time in your life and laugh your head off at what you wore and what you were into. And in twenty years, you'll think you were completely off your rocker."

"I bet I won't."

"Yes you will. And I can prove it."

"Whatever."

"Come with me."

"I'm in the middle of something here," Brett said, pointing at his game.

"Put it on pause and follow me, young man."

Sighing, Brett paused the game and followed his father to the attic.

"Any of this stuff look familiar?" Barry asked, pointing to the large trunk he'd just opened.

Inside the trunk was a scrapbook of photos, clothes, posters, and other assorted paraphernalia that used to be in Brett's room.

"I'd like you to take a moment and look over what you used to be into. What you used to wear. Now, try to imagine putting these posters back on your walls. Or wearing these clothes when your 'homeboys' come over to play some video games."

Brett laughed as he lifted a *Star Trek* outfit out of the trunk. "I can't believe I used to wear this."

"You didn't just wear it, you practically lived in it. And see this hat?" Barry said, picking up a Barney baseball cap. "You refused to take this hat off, even at night. You slept with it on. You used to cry if your mother or I tried to —"

"That's Jerrod," Brett said, in response to hearing the doorbell ring. Tossing the *Star Trek* outfit back in the trunk, he turned to leave. "I'm outta here, Dad."

"You sure you don't want to take your Barney cap with you?"

"Funny, Dad. I'll see you later."

"Hey, aren't you forgetting something?"

"What? Oh, crap. The bathroom."

"I'll tell Jerrod to wait for you."

Ten minutes later Jerrod and Brett were rolling east on Bloor Street in Jerrod's car, a not-so-new, souped-up, repainted Honda Civic he'd resurrected from his neighbour's driveway last fall. Jerrod had worked on it all winter, getting it running and then modifying, accessorising, and painting it with the money he'd made working as a dishwasher at Juice For Life.

"Ah, man, check out that chick over there," Jerrod said, pointing at a young woman standing on the street corner. "Homeless chicks are so hot."

Brett didn't respond. Instead, he let his gaze wander along Bloor West. Almost every day since he could remember he'd travelled up and down this street, observing the seasonal invasions and departures of U of T students, the openings and closings of countless shops and restaurants as well as the daily migration of neo-bohemians, writers, and soon-to-be famous musicians into the area. One of his favourite things to do was walk along Bloor Street, recording how his mood and attitude changed, how travelling from Bathurst to Spadina, for instance, made him feel artistic, free, and funky, like the best thing in the world he could do would be to grab a guitar and a journal, and hitchhike across North America. That was, until he continued to Avenue, walking east to Yonge and the ever-present symbols of prestige, power, and money — Bentleys, BMWs, Jaguars, and limousines parked outside shops like Harry Rosen and Holt Renfrew — made him want to be rich, made him want to get his MBA or go to law school so he could earn enough money to —

"So, man, what do you feel like doing?" Jerrod asked, interrupting his thoughts.

Brett shrugged. "Whatever."

"Yo, what's up with the sad face, man? The parental units on your ass again?"

"Naw. They're alright."

Well, at least one of them is, Brett thought to himself. His father was cool. As cool as someone who is forty could be. His mother, on the other hand, was another story. She drove him nuts. It was her hypocrisy more than anything. Here she was bitching about him not being responsible and living in "La-la Land" when every chance she got she was smoking marijuana.

He'd known about it since he was twelve. He was supposed to be at Jerrod's house for a sleepover but came back home and climbed the big maple tree in their backyard, waiting for his brothers and parents to go to sleep before he snuck back in the house. Just after the light went out in his parent's room, he saw his mother walk out onto the back deck and light up, the sweet, earthy scent wafting up to him through the branches and leaves. Over the past four years, he'd seen her smoking marijuana at least fifty times.

"Ladies. On the right," Jerrod said, gesturing to a small group of what looked to be university-aged women standing outside the Royal Conservatory of Music.

"Nice," Brett replied, trying to sound sincere.

Each time his mother gave Brett and his brothers her "Just Say No" to drugs speech, Brett had been tempted to throw her hypocrisy in her face, to say he knew about the stash she kept in her sock drawer, her twice weekly outings in the backyard after the rest of the family had gone to sleep. He never did, though. Just like he'd never use his mother's drug use as a justification for doing them. In fact, if anything, it was his reason not to do them. Despite the constant pressure from friends to try it, he was drug-free — something he was sure his mother wouldn't believe in a million years.

"Ah, man, I almost forgot," Jerrod said, smacking the steering wheel. "Check it out. Last night, me and Robbie are kickin' it along Yonge Street, and guess who we roll up on?"

Brett shrugged. "No idea."

"Josephine Bryant."

"Who?"

"Josephine Bryant. You know, that sweet-lookin' honey I told you we tried hookin' up with last year down at the CNE?"

"Doesn't ring a bell."

"You playin'?"

Brett shook his head. "Naw, man. I must've been out of it or something when you told me."

"It was that bitch who pretended she was really into me and Robbie and then, when Robbie suggested we continue the party back at his place, she started using all these big words and stuff and ditched us."

Brett started nodding his head. "Did she go to a private school or something?"

Jerrod nodded. "That's her. She went to Branksome Hall. Her parents were totally loaded."

"So, what, you and Robbie talked to her last night or something?"

"Talked to her? Dude, we banged her. Both of us. At the same time."

Brett gave Jerrod a look as if to say he thought Jerrod was full of shit.

"I'm serious, dude. We totally nailed her."

"Where?"

Jerrod flicked his thumb in the direction of the back seat. "In the back."

"Yeah, right. Whatever."

"I'm not lyin'. She took turns riding us. A few ups and downs on me. Then she'd shift over and do the same to Robbie. Then back over to me. It was like fuckin' a buckin' bronco or something."

Brett laughed. "Yeah, right. Maybe she was getting ready for the Calgary Stampede."

"Muthafuckah! You still don't believe me, do ya?"

Brett shrugged. "You gotta admit, Jer. It's a little far-fetched."

"Which is precisely why I taped it."

"What?"

"That's right. Because of doubting muthafuckahs just like you, I decided to tape the shit."

"You did not."

"Did too. I got the disk right here."

Jerrod produced a tiny digital disk from the car's console.

"You've got to be shittin' me."

"I'm not," Jerrod replied, grinning. "She's going to be our first star."

"Ah, man. That's crazy."

"No, that's real. As in real money in the bank. Which reminds me. You been thinking about what I told you last night?"

Jerrod was referring to his offer for Brett to join him in starting up an underage Internet porn site, complete with live, real-time, distribution feeds. He'd already told Brett he had several girls willing to do it.

"I don't know, man," Brett said. "I don't think it's for me."

"What are you talking about? This shit's tailor-made for you, my man. Tailor-made. I mean, look at you. With you in charge of recruiting we'll be able to get fifty chicks at our school alone. They practically drop their panties at the sight of you now, anyway. Hell, we're just giving them the chance to be like Paris and Pamela. Now why would you want to go and deny them that opportunity?"

Brett chuckled. "What about Juice For Life?"

"I quit that shit."

"What? Are you kidding? I thought you loved it there?"

"Past tense, my man. Past tense. The way I see it, as soon as we get this Internet thing going, I'll be making enough money to — yo, yo, yo. Check it out," Jerrod said, slowing the car down and pointing in the direction of two young girls walking with a woman on the other side of the street in front of Harry Rosen. "Speak of the devils. See the one on the right there? She's already signed up."

Brett recognised her immediately. She went to the same school as Brett and Jerrod. "Ah, man. Her? You're kidding, right?"

Jerrod shook his head and honked the horn. "Yo, ladies, whassup?"

* * * * * * * * * * * . To Be Continued . . .

you get used to it . . . .

"Hello, *boys!*"

"Girls!" Geena shouted, watching in horror as her fourteen-year-old daughter Kimberley and Kimberley's new best friend, Penelope, struck suggestive poses and blew kisses at the two men in the passing car.

"Relax, mother," Kimberley said. "We know them. They're from our school."

"They're from your school? They look a lot older than that."

"They're like only seventeen."

"Still, you shouldn't be acknowledging them in that manner."

"Completely harmless, mother. Besides, it's not as though we want to have sex with them or —"

"Oh. My. God. Look at that," Penelope said.

"What?"

"That," Penelope said, pointing at the picture of a middle-aged bikini-clad actress at the beach, a bright red circle enclosing the offending region, highlighting the cellulite.

Geena rolled her eyes. Two months ago, around the same time Kimberley started hanging out with Penelope, the tabloids had become required reading for her daughter. Since then, she'd find Kimberley eagerly reading them, clipping the photos and pasting them up in her bedroom, cutting out the headlines and sticking them in Geena's purse or on her "Things to Do List."

"Ugh," Kimberley was now saying. "Cellulite. Gross."

"Is there anything worse?"

"Doubtful."

"Like, please, someone, explain to me why she'd want to wear something like that?"

"Maybe because she's at the beach," Geena suggested.

"Excuse me?" Penelope said, giving Kimberley a look as if to say, 'Why is your mother talking to us?'

Kimberley glared at her mother, hoping she'd get the hint. She'd made her mother promise before Penelope came over that she wouldn't speak to her or Penelope during the walk to the Yonge and Bloor subway station. She was tired of her mother embarrassing her in front of her friends. "Mother," she was now saying, shaking her head at Geena. "I thought we had a deal?"

"What? The poor woman's at the beach. What do you guys expect her to wear?"

"Maybe something that doesn't show all that gross cellulite," Penelope replied.

Geena smiled. "Just wait. You'll have cellulite, too, one day."

Penelope snickered. "Yeah, right. By the time we're that age, they'll already have a cure."

"I didn't realise cellulite was a disease."

Kimberley groaned. "Mother. Can you please get your own conversation?"

"Sorry," Geena replied, sighing. Then, a few moments later, as they were walking past Starbucks inside Chapters, she recognised her friend, Beth Chambers, seated inside. "Oh, I see a friend. I think I'll go in and say hi before my meeting."

"Who is it?" Kimberley snapped, sounding suspicious, quickly scanning the inside of the coffee shop.

Ever since Geena and Kimberley's father divorced last year, Kimberley had been on the lookout for her father's replacement — and doing her best to ensure Geena remained single. She consistently erased messages left for Geena on their home voicemail or informed the men who called that her mother was back with her father now. Whenever Geena brought a date home, Kimberley would pounce on the poor man the moment he came through the front door, immediately relating some hideous story of incest or mental illness or physical abuse, effectively sabotaging any chance Geena had of furthering the relationship. It had gotten to the point where Kimberley's antics had forced Geena to be far more creative in her search for a potential partner.

"Don't worry, it's not a man," Geena said, "It's only Beth Chambers. Someone who doesn't actually mind if I speak to her. Can you girls manage the rest of the way?"

"Of course we can, Mother."

"Are you sure?"

Kimberley rolled her eyes. "It's not like this is our first time on the subway. We take it, like, every day."

"Yes, I know. But it's getting late."

"Mother, we've been over this a million times already."

Geena nodded. Regretfully she'd made a deal with Kimberley that when she turned fourteen she would be allowed to go to the late showing of movies. This was in response to Kimberley badgering Geena non-stop for nearly two months, telling her that all her other friends' parents had been letting them go to the late show since they were thirteen. "You have your cell phone on you, right, Kimberley?"

"Yes."

"Okay. Well, call if you need a ride or if anything happens or if —"

"Goodbye, mother. Have fun at your meeting."

"Okay. Thanks. Be careful, girls."

Geena continued watching Kimberley and Penelope walking along Bloor West for a few moments before entering Starbucks and heading straight for her friend. "Hey," she said, plopping down on the chair across the table for two from Beth.

"Geena. Oh, hi. How are you?"

"I'll live. You?"

"Great."

"You here by yourself?"

Beth shook her head and smiled, pointing to the line-up. "I'm here with Bethany. She's ordering for us."

"Ah, that's sweet," Geena said, glancing at Bethany, noticing she was dressed in the same clothes as her mother, complete with a white bow in her long, dark hair. "How old is she now?"

"She's seven."

"Seven," Geena cooed, nostalgically, recalling Kimberley at seven. "Seven is a wonderful age. They still adore you at seven."

"She's my little angel," Beth replied, waving and smiling at Bethany.

"Well, all I can say is, enjoy it while you can. You only have another few years before she starts telling you she hates your guts and wishes you were dead."

"Excuse me?"

Geena nodded. "It's true. Kimberley was twelve when she started with her attitude."

"I don't think Bethany's going to be like that."

"Trust me, I didn't think Kimberley would be either. Boy, was I naive. We used to be best friends. We did everything together. Went grocery shopping, clothes shopping, hung out in malls, went to the movies. We baked cookies and cooked dinner together. Went for picnics. Read *Harry Potter* and V.C. Andrews books together. Then, three weeks after her twelfth birthday, I became the enemy. Almost overnight I became uncool. Boring. Out of style. Stupid. Old. Nothing I did was right. She couldn't stand to even be seen with me. And she finally told me she hated me."

"That's horrible."

"I know. It tore my heart out."

"I couldn't imagine Bethany saying those kinds of things," Beth said, turning her head and looking at her daughter, obviously unconvinced her little angel could be capable of such behaviour.

"Of course, the real tragedy is that she's influencing her younger sister. Drew's only nine but she's already starting to act like her older sister."

"Well, I really don't know what to say except you seem to be holding up okay."

Geena smiled. "The sad part is you get used to it. The snide remarks, the silent contempt, the disparaging glares — everything."

"Really?"

Geena sighed. "I didn't think I would, but I have."

"I don't know if I could."

"You will. Trust me. You'll have to or you'll never survive."

The two women turned to look at Bethany. She was next in line to place her order. "So, how do you cope?" Beth asked, winking at Bethany.

Geena smiled, wanly. "I keep telling myself that it will pass. That I was just like her when I was her age. My mother was my life until the year I went into grade nine and then that was it. I hated her until I graduated from college. So, I take refuge in knowing her contempt won't last forever. Plus I've had a voice-activated translator installed in my brain so whenever Kimberley tells me to go to hell or to fuck off all I hear is, 'I love you, Mommy,' or, 'You're the best Mommy ever.' And, of course, I watch a lot of *Dr. Phil.*"

"That guy's an idiot!"

. . . . **To Be Continued . . .**

are you hearing any of this?

"*Rawnie*," Lance said, cringing while quickly surveying the coffee shop to see if the two women, or anyone else, for that matter, had heard what Rawnie had just said.

"Well, it's true."

"Oh, come now. It is not. Dr. Phil helps people."

"How? How does he help people?"

"By getting people to know themselves better. By giving them the tools to analyse their thoughts and feelings so they can gain more control over their lives."

"That's precisely the problem."

"How is *that* the problem?"

"Because we already know ourselves far too well. Guys like Dr. Phil are a virus. They infect us with the idea that it's okay to spend all our time examining ourselves. In the process, they make people so overly obsessed with thinking about themselves they're in danger of drowning in a narcissistic pool."

"I think you might be exaggerating just a —"

"You know who I blame for all this?"

"Who, my dear?"

"Newton."

"Newton? You mean, Sir Isaac Newton?"

Rawnie nodded. "He's the one who said the universe resembled a clockwork mechanism and that if we studied all the parts and knew how they worked we'd be able to figure out how the entire universe worked. Ever since then, we've been sharpening our analytical hatchets and hacking away at things, deconstructing everything — including ourselves — in a vain attempt to understand how it all works."

"So, now you're saying that the *examined* life is not worth living?"

"No, I'm saying the *over*-examined life is not worth living. For the same reason we can't stare at the stars without immediately wondering what this or that star is called, we can't look into someone else's eyes without wondering what they're thinking or feeling. And why? Why can't we just look at something or someone without this irritating impulse to figure it out, without these annoying grasps at analysis? Because of Sir Isaac Newton, the father of deconstructionism. He's the reason we over-examine and over-analyse everything."

Lance smiled. "Rawnie, as much as I'm interested in your fabulous theories, I didn't invite you down from dear old Hamilton to hear them. I'm interested in knowing how things are progressing."

"With what?"

"Not with what, my dear. With whom."

"When did you start this annoying habit of calling everyone 'dear'?"

"The moment I turned twenty-six," Lance sniffed. "I suddenly realised I was closer to thirty than twenty and promptly felt old."

"Lance, twenty-six is not old."

"For a gay man in Toronto, I'm considered almost over-the-hill."

"You're insane."

"And you're avoiding my question."

"Which one?"

"Don't play coy with me, my dear."

"Stop calling me that. And, for your information, I have no idea how it's going. One minute I think William's a complete letch, the most uninhibited, maladjusted, mysterious weirdo I've ever encountered, and the next, I think he's sweet, naive, charming, and boyish."

"So, you're in love, then?"

"No. Certainly not. I'm . . . I'm in*trigued*."

"Are you hearing any of this?"

. . . . To Be Continued . . .

she's married . . . .

While standing in line behind a young girl with a bright white bow in her hair, Hilary Brackenbush had been dividing her time between a) eye-flirting with a very tall, very muscular black man sipping an iced cappuccino, b) scanning the café to see who else was noticing her, and c) assessing her most recent protegé, Amelia DeSantos.

Each time she glanced at Amelia, Hilary felt a slight twinge of envy: Amelia looked fabulous. Of course, much of this could be attributed to the spray-on tan and new hairstyle Hilary suggested Amelia get, as well as the slimming effect of Amelia's new sleeveless sundress which Hilary had not only picked out for her but insisted she buy, even though she knew Amelia couldn't afford it.

To Hilary, Amelia was just another in a long list of faux friends she had successfully convinced to live beyond her means, concluding it was merely an unavoidable fact of life for any modern-day woman — until she found herself a substantially solvent BFH (boyfriend-fiancé-husband) to replace her well-travelled Visa card.

Besides, Hilary said to herself, once again returning her gaze to the muscular man, no matter how fabulous Amelia looks in her new outfit, her hair is still too frizzy and her cleavage merely the result of the Victoria Secret Sensual Shaper bra she's wearing.

Of course, if this wasn't enough to console Hilary, she had only to remind herself of the fact that Amelia, now only two months away from her thirty-fifth birthday, was still hopelessly single, while she, a year younger, had successfully married one of Toronto's most eligible bachelors, Sheldon Bronstein, six months ago.

"Am I hearing any of what?" Hilary eventually responded, sounding annoyed.

"What that woman's been saying," Amelia said, raising her arm and pointing at the woman dressed in cargo shorts, a black tank top, and a pair of ratty sandals. "Over there. On the other side of the fireplace."

After removing her eyes from the muscular man and gazing in the direction of Amelia's still pointing finger, Hilary suddenly grabbed Amelia's arm. "Don't point," she said, her tone serious, almost chastising. "In fact, don't even look."

"Why not?" Amelia replied, looking more than slightly bewildered.

"I don't want her to see us," Hilary whispered. "I know her."

"You know her?"

Hilary nodded. "Unfortunately."

"Who is she?"

"Rawnie DeVrais."

"Oh my God. *That's* Rawnie DeVrais? Are you sure?"

"Of course I'm sure."

"Wow. I had no idea she was so . . . so —"

"Obnoxious? She's the most obnoxious woman you'll ever meet."

Amelia was going to say "beautiful." She'd first heard of Rawnie DeVrais while attending a house party downtown late last summer. Two women were discussing her, describing how ingenious and influential and alluring she was, how her random acts of civil disobedience had inspired people around the globe, how she'd become a role model for millions. Since Amelia had never heard of Rawnie DeVrais, she'd concluded the woman was nothing more than a figment of someone's imagination or an urban legend at best.

Now, standing only a few metres from her, Amelia could sense Rawnie's influence, how the mere sight of Rawnie's nondescript clothing, her bare taut arms, and her short, unstyled hair made Amelia suddenly feel ashamed to be wearing designer clothes, a fake tan, and the latest hairstyle.

Almost immediately Amelia began calculating how long it would take to pay off what Hilary had deemed "essential items for any sensible woman," silently scolding herself for not standing up to Hilary, for not telling her that she had more pressing and prudent things to purchase. Like an air conditioner for her apartment. Or the complete works of William Shakespeare. Or a new set of brakes for her car. Amelia glared at Hilary, hating her for being so persuasive.

"Did you just wink at that guy?" she asked Hilary, referring to the tall, muscular guy seated with his two buddies at a nearby table.

Hilary nodded.

"Why?"

"Why not?"

"Um, maybe because you're married."

"So?"

"So? Why would you — wait a second. Where's your ring?"

"In my purse."

"What's it doing there?"

"It's too cumbersome."

The truth was Hilary rarely wore her ring in public when she wasn't with Sheldon, believing the sight of her ringless left hand gave other men hope, implanting the idea that they might have a chance to be with her. "Relax, Amelia. I'm just having some fun."

"Yeah, at Sheldon's expense."

"I'm sure Sheldon's having his fun, too."

"Hilary, Sheldon's the most faithful guy in the world."

"I know. And he really enjoys being that way. And I really enjoy flirting."

"Does he know?"

"That I flirt?"

"And take off your ring when you're not with him?"

"Of course not."

"That's what I thought."

"Where are you going?"

"The washroom," Amelia said, heading for the entrance to Chapters bookstore, stating, "She's married," in a pleasant but firm voice as she passed by the tall, muscular man.

. . . . To Be Continued . . .

I prefer Don Cherry

"Thank you," Wayne called after the woman, watching her walk into Chapters. Then, kicking Peter under the table, he said. "Now, can we get down to it?"

"Hey, it's not like you can blame me," Peter replied, easing back in his chair. "The woman's been giving me some serious eye contact ever since she came in. She even winked at me."

Frank shook his head. "Did you not hear her friend? She's married. She probably gets her kicks from leading men like you on."

"Speaking of leading men," Wayne said, "can we —"

"Yeah, yeah, yeah. I heard you the first time. Where were we?"

"I was saying that I'm way more Canadian than you."

Peter gave a final glance at the woman he'd been flirting with, noticing she was now smiling at an older gentleman seated at the table next to theirs, then returned his attention to Wayne. "More Canadian than me, eh?"

Wayne nodded.

"You're crazy, pal. No one, I mean, *no one*, is more Canadian than me."

"Prove it."

"What? How?"

Wayne shrugged. "We can run down a list of things that we think makes us Canadian. And Frank here can judge which one of us is more quintessentially Canadian."

"Guys. Maybe this isn't the time or the place for this," Frank said, looking around at the rest of the patrons in the small café.

"Oh, I think it is," replied Wayne.

"So do I," agreed Peter.

"Well, then let's have it, Mr. Canadiana," Wayne said.

"You want me to start?"

"The stage is yours."

"Okay, well, for starters, I was born in Ottawa, Canada's capital."

"Yeah, well, I was born in Toronto, the most famous Canadian city in the world."

"I went to Upper Canada College."

"As did I."

"I went to the University of Ottawa. Again, in our nation's capital."

"I attended the University of Toronto. Again, located in the most famous Canadian city in the world."

"I have a degree in Political Science, and specialised in Canadian Politics and Domestic Affairs."

"I have a Master's degree in Canadian History with a minor in French."

"I'm fluent in English *and* French."

"I'm fluent in English, French, *and* Ojibway."

"I spent a summer in British Columbia with the Haida-Gwai."

"I spent two summers on the Six Nations reserve when I was in high school, working at the Iroquois Lodge."

"I've had sex while shooting a section of rapids on the Ottawa River."

"My wife and I conceived our first child in a canoe on Tom Thomson Lake in Algonquin Park."

"I know how to make bannock."

"I prepared it last week for my wife who, I might add, is French-Canadian."

"My father, who *I* might add, is English-Canadian, served our country in the Korean War."

"My grandfather served our country in the Second World War. He helped liberate France."

"My great-grandfather served in the First World War."

"Where?"

"He was part of the contingent of Canadian soldiers who most historians agree was the most significant battle in Canadian history — Vimy Ridge."

"How can you say that?"

"Because it's true. Take a poll. Read a Pierre Berton book. You'll see."

"Speaking of Mr. Berton, he's my favourite author."

"I'm partial to Margaret Atwood and Margaret Laurence."

"I drink *Canadian* beer."

"I prefer *Canadian Club* whiskey."

"I shop at Sears."

"I shop at The Bay."

"I have an authentic beaver hat from the Hudson's Bay Company."

"I have an authentic Hudson's Bay credit card."

"Our family has a cottage in Muskoka."

"Our family vacations in Whistler, Banff, or Fernie in the winter and Halifax, Montreal, or Calgary in the summer."

"I own a pair of snowshoes."

"I actually *use* my pair, not as a decoration on the wall above my fireplace like you do but as a means of transportation. Every winter my wife and I go winter camping in a different provincial park."

"I've seen the petroglyphs in Lake Superior Park."

"I was a canoe ranger in Quetico, saw the pictographs, and climbed 'Warrior Rock.'"

"I've been to every province and territory in our country."

"I've paddled a kayak from Vancouver Island to the Great Lakes one summer. And from the Great Lakes to Newfoundland the next."

"Bullshit."

"It's true. You can ask my wife. She came with me."

"Speaking of wives, I proposed to my wife on Canada Day."

"I proposed to my wife on the day we arrived on the shores of Newfoundland. Which happened to be the anniversary of the day the province joined Confederation and made our country complete."

"My favourite movie is *Lives of the Saints*."

"Mine is *Black Robe*."

"My favourite TV station is CBC."

"My favourite radio station is CBC Radio One."

"My favourite show is *Hockey Night in Canada*."

"Mine is *The Red Green Show*."

"I was on *Reach for the Top*."

"I was an extra for *Degrassi*."

"My favourite hockey team is the Toronto Maple Leafs."

"Mine is the Montreal Canadiens. Notice the emphasis on *Canadiens*."

"I think Peter Mansbridge is Canada's best anchorman."

"I prefer Don Cherry."

"Don Cherry isn't an anchorman. He's a moron."

"I'm certain millions of hockey fans across the nation would disagree with you on that one."

"I read the *Globe and Mail*."

"I read the *National Post*."

"I —"

"Excuse me. I'm terribly sorry to interrupt you gentlemen, but did I overhear you say you were a canoe ranger in Quetico Provincial Park?"

* * * * * * * * * * * * **To Be Continued . . .**

the usual tension . . . .

For nearly an hour, Manuel had been staring out the window of Starbucks, casually observing the pedestrian and vehicular traffic zipping along Bloor West, watching with only mild interest as a traffic cop wrote up a ticket and tucked it under the windshield wiper of his Jaguar, adding it to the two tickets already there. He'd just decided to go for a stroll when he overheard the tall, muscular man say he'd been a ranger in Quetico Provincial Park.

"Yes you did," replied the muscular man.

"When?"

"When what?"

"When were you in Quetico?"

"Oh, I've never been. We were just rehearsing for a play we're going to start workshopping next week."

"I see," said Manuel, trying not to sound too disappointed. "Well, then, my sincere apologies for the interruption, gentlemen."

After encouraging the men to carry on with their performance, Manuel got up from his table and walked quickly into Chapters. While browsing the books in a bin near the front of the store, the sight of Jon Krakauer's *Into the Wild* caused him to retreat into a memory, immediately recalling the moment his son, Darryl, told him he was going on another trip.

"How long are you planning on going for?" he'd asked, watching Darryl stuffing a sleeping bag into his backpack.

"A month, maybe longer."

"Where to this time?"

"Quetico, I think."

Manuel had long ago acknowledged that Darryl was different than most boys. One look at the bookshelf in his room, filled with the likes of Henry David Thoreau, John Muir, Sigurd Olson, David Thompson, Bob Henderson, Bill Mason, Susanna Moodie, and Grey Owl was evidence of this difference. Not to mention the fact that while most boys his age spent their spring breaks at Daytona Beach or the summer after graduating university backpacking across Europe, Darryl was busy exploring Canada.

From a relatively early age, he maintained he had little interest in visiting other countries until he'd actually seen his own. "In fact," he'd told Manuel recently, "there's enough geography and history in Canada that I doubt I'll be needing a passport any time soon."

The only thing that initially concerned Manuel was that his son always travelled alone. Of course, as Darryl was quick to point out, "There aren't too many people really interested in doing what I do, Dad. The closest most people want to get to exploring Canada is going up north to a cottage in Muskoka for a long weekend in the summer or skiing Whistler and Blue Mountain in the winter."

These differences in the degrees of exploration that Darryl referred to were what led to his mother leaving Manuel. They had met in Burlington, in a specialty wood store. She was buying wood to build a canoe; he was there to write an article on the store for the *Spectator*. They got to talking, talking led to dinner, dinner led to more talking. Each found the other fascinating. She was a nature buff and loved the outdoors — canoeing, hiking, horseback riding, snowshoeing, kayaking, camping. He was far more urban-oriented, preferring cafés to canoes, treadmills to forest trails, the Four Seasons hotel to the four seasons of Canada. Despite their seemingly incompatible constitutions, however, they married three months later, convinced that marrying someone with their own interests would make for a very boring union.

They stayed together long enough for Darryl to not only acquire a latent taste for the outdoors but also to be old enough to make the informed decision to remain in Toronto with his father when they divorced. The day following Darryl's decision, his mother left, leaving behind a note for Darryl, explaining that she could no longer fit herself into the city, that she required an ongoing communion with the land, that their twice-monthly weekend visits to their cottage in Muskoka during the summer months were not enough to sate her desire to, as Thoreau had so aptly put it, "suck the marrow out of life." She left no forwarding address.

For a time, perhaps out of anger or resentment towards her, Darryl immersed himself in Toronto, embracing the city so completely he even refused to visit the cottage. As he grew older, however, he slowly lost his desire to remain solely within the city's limits.

The first evidence of this was a collect phone call Manuel received from Darryl the summer before he enrolled in university. It was a Sunday afternoon. Manuel was at the cottage with a lady friend, packing up, getting ready to return to Toronto. When Darryl told him where he was, Manuel was quite surprised.

"What the hell are you doing in Sault Ste. Marie, son?"

Apparently, instead of returning to work after lunch on Friday, he'd continued past the office building on Yonge Street where he was working and, two days of walking and hitchhiking later, found himself in the Soo.

"I can't believe how many stories I heard along the way," he'd told Manuel. "The people I've met are great. The last guy to pick me up thought he knew Mom. He said he was pretty sure a friend of his paddled with her in Kilarney Park."

As these impromptu excursions became the norm — and longer in duration — there developed another cause for Manuel to be concerned: with each return to Toronto, Darryl's re-entry into city life became increasingly difficult. Initially, Manuel thought it was nothing more than the usual tension associated with leaving the solitude and serenity of self-directed travel and returning to the agenda of a major, modern city. But, recently, this transition tension had intensified, making Manuel acutely aware of the possibility that one of these days,

Darryl might decide not to return to the city.

Still standing in front of the book bin, now holding *Into the Wild* in his hand, Manuel once again pulled Darryl's journal from his shoulder satchel. The journal had arrived two weeks ago, instead of Darryl. After opening it, Manuel turned to where he'd left off and began re-reading the last entry:

"Today I am paddling to a sacred place in Quetico Park called Warrior Rock, a place renowned for its simple yet devastating rite of passage for those natives that once called this area home. Deceptively serene from a distance, its slope grows more formidable and menacing as each stroke of the paddle draws me nearer. Sitting in my canoe, staring up at this large chunk of Canadian Shield erupting out of the water, it is not difficult to imagine the skinned knees, broken bones, scraped hands, and the blood of hundreds of men soaking into the rock and water as they tried over and over to climb to the top. I will spend however long it takes trying to accomplish what these young men did hundreds of years ago. Before nightfall, I hope to —"

"Excuse me, sir. Are going to buy that book?"

. . . . **To Be Continued . . .**

circa 1984 × × × × × × × × × × × × × ×

Alternately looking from Dennis to the journal in his hand with a slightly confused expression, the man didn't respond until Dennis gestured to the book tucked beneath the journal.

"Oh, I'm sorry. I thought you were referring to this," the man said, motioning to the journal. Then, after stuffing the journal into his satchel, he tapped the book's cover a couple of times and said, "It's one of my son's favourites."

"Mine, too," Lauren said.

"Is that so?"

Lauren nodded. "Have you read it?"

The man shook his head. "Unfortunately, no. Not yet."

"Oh, you should. It's quite good."

The man turned the book over in his hands a couple of times, slowly nodding his head. "You know something, I think I'll take your advice and buy it," he said, smiling at Lauren.

"I guarantee you won't be disappointed."

"Thank you," the man said, starting to walk away.

"My pleasure."

Dennis took a moment to watch the man move in the direction of the checkout counter. "Well, I certainly hope that wasn't the last copy," he said, turning to Lauren.

"Why?"

"Because that was the book my grandfather wanted."

"Oh. Really? I didn't . . . well, I'm sure there's more than just one copy in the store."

Dennis sighed and started scanning the book bin. "There'd better be."

"Why? What's the big deal?"

Dennis hesitated. "Okay, I didn't want to tell you this, but once a week he sends me to a different bookstore in the city to buy him a book and if I don't get it at the store he requested it from he gets really upset."

Lauren raised her eyebrows. "That's kind of bizarre, isn't it?"

"*That's* my grandfather. Shit, there are no more copies here."

"Maybe the guy didn't get it from this bin," Lauren suggested. "Maybe it's on a shelf somewhere."

"Damn," Dennis said, already on his way to one of the computer terminals to check the in-store stock. "I should've just grabbed it from the guy when I had the chance. Or bribed him."

"I'm sorry, Dennis. Really. I didn't know."

"Don't worry about it," Dennis said, sighing. "It's not your fault. I should've said something. Besides, I'm just glad you agreed to come with me. Especially on such short notice."

Last night, Dennis, after learning that Lauren was coming to Toronto for the weekend, had asked her to accompany him to visit his grandfather and employer, Mr. Henri Easton.

"It's no problem," Lauren was now saying. "Anything for a friend. Besides, the more I hear about your grandfather, the more interesting he sounds."

Dennis chuckled. On the way to the bookstore, he had explained to Lauren that he'd spent most of the last five years in the employ of his grandfather, performing all sorts of odd jobs and running countless errands, in exchange for a stipend that amounted to slightly more than the current minimum wage standard. After paying for rent, food, and utilities, the small stipend left him with barely enough money to make the minimum interest payment on his substantial student loan debt.

"Trust me," Dennis said. "He's not interesting. He's just a crusty, senile, S.O.B. who treats me like a servant."

"If he's so awful, why do you continue working for him?"

"Because he's also rich. Filthy rich."

"So, what, you're looking for an inheritance or something?"

Dennis nodded. "I figure if I put up with his crap long enough, when he finally kicks, I'll be set. Besides, he's let it slip that my name is already on a few things."

"Like what?"

"His cigar collection, for starters. And this really ornate, antique, solid oak writing desk. And a handwoven, Persian rug that dates back to the fourteenth century."

"Wow."

"I plan on selling the desk and the rug to an antique dealer. I've already talked to a few of them. I could get anywhere from eight to ten thousand dollars for the pair."

"Wouldn't your grandfather want you to keep these things?"

Dennis smiled. "I plan on keeping the cigars. Besides, who cares? He'll be dead. He won't know. Plus, for all the work I do for him, I'll consider it a — shit!"

"What?"

"There are no more copies left at this store. That guy got the last one."

"Really?"

Dennis nodded. "I wouldn't doubt it if my grandfather knew there was only one copy left when he called me last night to tell me where to get the book. Hell, it wouldn't surprise me if he hired that guy to buy the last one just as we entered the store."

"You really think he'd go to all that trouble?"

Dennis nodded. "He would if he thought it might teach me a lesson."

"Look," Lauren said, pointing at the computer monitor. "They have two copies at Indigo in the Eaton Centre. And two more at the Chapters downtown. Why don't we just grab a copy from one of these stores? I'm sure he won't mind."

Just as Dennis was about to reveal what had happened the first and last time he had attempted to do such a thing, he saw the man they'd been talking to earlier exiting the store. "I'm going to ask that guy if I can buy his copy," he said, starting to run after the man.

Ten minutes later, seated in the passenger seat of Lauren's car, anxiously tapping his feet on the floorboard, Dennis wanted to scream like a madman in response to being hopelessly mired in gridlock traffic. At the moment, Lauren's car, southbound on Yonge, was blocking the Bloor Street crosswalk — the result of a large delivery truck's decision to suddenly break down, effectively pinning Lauren's car between the pick-up truck in front of her and the convertible Mini Cooper behind her. Jammed up behind the Mini Cooper, a large SUV, partially blocking eastbound traffic on Bloor Street, was receiving a near-constant barrage of noisy reprimands. Each time someone honked or shouted something at the SUV, the driver would flip his finger out the window and blast his horn.

"Unbefuckinglievable," Dennis said, shaking his head in response to his misfortune.

In his rush to get to the exit of Chapters, he'd bumped into a young girl with a white bow in her hair, spilling the apple juice she was holding onto her dress. He'd then spent the next minute or so alternately apologising to the girl and her identically dressed mother and watching the man with the book removing a handful of parking tickets from the windshield of his Jaguar before getting in and pulling away from the curb. And now, ten minutes later, here he was, stuck in a traffic jam, receiving irate glares from the countless pedestrians struggling to get around Lauren's car while being serenaded by a near continuous harangue of honking horns.

A split second before Dennis was about to yell at the guy in the SUV to stop honking his goddamned horn, he saw his cousin, Maggie, walking towards him along the Bloor Street sidewalk. Almost immediately the corner of his upper lip began to curl. The thought of talking to Maggie right now increased his already substantial level of irritation.

Maggie was his grandfather's only other grandchild and the person Dennis considered to be his main competition in the inheritance sweepstakes. As Maggie drew nearer, however, joining the rest of the gathered throng on the corner of Bloor and Yonge waiting for the light to change, Dennis realised it wasn't her, just someone who dressed like her — right down to her black boots, blue plaid skirt, white blouse, and dyed dirty blonde hair tied up in several ribbons, the way Madonna used to, circa 1984.

When the light changed and the throng advanced, immediately bottlenecking and queuing up to squeeze single-file between the bumpers of the cars blocking the intersection, Dennis noticed, with increasing interest, that instead of joining one of the lines, the Maggie look-alike was walking directly at Lauren's car. A moment later, without breaking stride, she hopped onto the hood of the car, waggled what looked to be a bagged bottle of wine at Dennis and Lauren as she walked across the hood, then jumped down on the other side of the car and continued walking along the crosswalk, cheered on by the less brazen pedestrians.

. . . . **To Be Continued** . . .

c'est magnifique

Alfred North Whitehead once said there are moments in our lives when we suffer from a deficiency of language, when we're unable to explain what we're feeling. Josephine Bryant knew exactly what Mr. Whitehead meant: ever since she was told she had an inoperable brain tumour, the feelings produced by this news had continually eluded her descriptive grasp.

This annoyed Josephine immensely.

Despite realising, with the help of Mr. Whitehead, that certain feelings shied away from explanation, that some sensations stubbornly refused to be corralled by words, she had always prided herself on her ability to find the correct word or phrase for any given experience.

She derived this pride, in part, from having spent the summer before her parents enrolled her in Branksome Hall, a private girls' school, reading a dictionary and a thesaurus. Her siblings, especially her older sister, thought it extremely pretentious that a thirteen-year-old girl was engaged in such activity and often told Josephine she should go back to reading her *Harry Potter* books. Using an increasingly imaginative array of expletives and accompanying adjectives, Josephine would tell her sister what she thought of her and promptly return to reading her dictionary.

Each day she'd test out the new words, incorporating them into her day-to-day conversations, carefully monitoring the impression they made on her listeners. She began striking up conversations with almost anyone — bank managers, lawyers, mechanics, nurses, construction workers, sales clerks — often using terms and words confined to their field, talking in "lawyer-speak" or "doctor-speak" as Josephine liked to call it.

Within a few weeks she was speaking at a level that embarrassed her friends and siblings, where, in conversation with them, she either had to dumb-down her language to be understood or recite a list of increasingly simplistic synonyms for some of the words she was using until a spark of comprehension came into their eyes. Although a few people, such as her older sister, were irritated by her ever-expanding vocabulary, others were mesmerised by it, often regarding Josephine as though she possessed a rare and beautiful gift.

By her sixteenth birthday, Josephine's vocabulary had become so extensive and so advanced, that her descriptions of the emotions and events experienced by others were often far superior to their own. By putting their experiences into her words, she not only gave them a reality their owners were incapable of providing, her reinterpretation often became their reality.

It wasn't long after realising she had the power to profoundly alter peoples' perceptions with the clever use of language that Josephine began reinterpreting her own reality, subtly altering and reorganising the outside world within her mind, content to exist in this increasingly isolated, re-imagined reality.

Until she received the news of the tumour.

Until then, Josephine assumed she would never be at a loss for words, that her three-year, self-directed study of the dictionary and thesaurus had virtually guaranteed she would always be able to encapsulate any experience with words — as well as enable her to verbally manipulate that experience to create a different reality for herself.

Undoubtedly it was this mistaken assumption that had caused Josephine, in those first few days after finding out about the tumour, to be so annoyed — both by her inability to describe what she was feeling as well as her inability to reinterpret these feelings.

Her doctor had told her the tumour, located deep inside her occipital lobe, was growing. Slowly. Grudgingly slow. But it was growing, nonetheless. He'd said it would only be a matter of months, possibly just a few weeks before it would start affecting her sight. Complete blindness was inevitable. Then seizures. A coma. And death.

Of course, there had been moments since getting the news when Josephine thought she'd done it, when she was certain she'd finally found the right combination of words, but then, as little as a minute later, these same words would seem lifeless and ineffectual, vacuous imitations of the sensations throbbing through her. It was why, a few weeks ago, she'd stopped reading the dictionary and the thesaurus and started talking like an average sixteen-year-old girl. It was also why she decided to leave home.

Before she lost her eyesight, Josephine wanted to experience the world, really experience it, like a baby would — without words, without the word's ability to manipulate reality. She wanted to let in as much raw, unedited, undiluted life as she could bear. In two weeks she felt she'd experienced more and lived more than most people do in a lifetime.

After the brief detour over the hood of the car, Josephine walked up Yonge Street before making a right onto Roxborough Avenue, en route to what had become her favourite eatery, a quaint, out-of-the-way establishment catering to a very select clientele. She'd even brought her own bottle of wine for the occasion, uncorking and tasting it prior to leaving.

David, the evening's maitre d' and designated lookout, was outside the establishment, having a cigarette and gazing wistfully at the richly coloured evening sky. When he saw Josephine he immediately smiled and stepped towards her.

"Josephine, my dear," he said, embracing her and air-kissing both cheeks. "How are you?"

"I am well," Josephine replied, returning David's air kisses.

"Do you have a reservation?"

"Um, no. Is that a problem?"

David nodded. "I am afraid it's already full."

"How long is the wait?"

David pulled pensively on his scruffy beard. "Fifteen, maybe twenty minutes."

"That long?"

"It is well worth the wait. There's something in there to please everyone's palate — leftover pad Thai, mango chicken, honey-braised ham, *salade de fruits,* and a wide assortment of almost-fresh baguettes."

"What do you recommend?"

"Tough call. I had a little bit of everything earlier and it was all very good."

"Well, I think I'll have the honey-braised ham with an almost-fresh baguette," Josephine replied, after a moment's deliberation. "It will go well with my wine."

"May I?" David asked, gesturing towards her bottle of wine.

"Of course," Josephine said, quickly pulling it from the bag and easing out the cork.

"Ah, *c'est magnifique,*" David said after downing a large gulp. Then, handing the bottle back to Josephine, he said, "If you'd like, I could go in and get you something to go? You could have your dinner in the park."

Josephine took a minute to consider David's proposal, then shook her head. "I'd prefer to dine in. Are you sure I can't squeeze in somewhere?"

"Follow me. I will show you how busy it is. You can see for yourself." Taking hold of David's hand, Josephine allowed him to escort her into the establishment.

"I can't believe she actually said that to you."

. . . . **To Be Continued . . .**

too civilised · · · · · · · · · · · · · · ·

Bonnie shrugged. "She was probably just having a bad day."

After glancing at the maitre d' assisting a woman down the makeshift stairs into the dumpster, Janine turned back to Bonnie. "A bad day? Bonnie, you're incredible, you know that?" Janine stared at her friend in disbelief. "I don't know a single person who has endured more adversity than you and yet you always find an excuse for other people's cruelty."

Bonnie continued carefully cutting along the edge of a partly eaten section of ham with her pocket knife, making certain she was at least a centimetre from the previous diner's leftover teeth marks. "It's not an excuse if it's true," she said, scraping the discarded section of ham off her paper plate before opening up a packet of salt and sprinkling it on the remaining ham.

Janine regarded Bonnie for a long moment, mentally inventorying the list of hardships her friend had endured: an abusive father; an alcoholic and absentee mother; four foster homes; two failed marriages; a nervous breakdown at age twenty-four after her first divorce; a month-long stint in the psychiatric hospital and a two-year diet of anti-depressants and weekly therapy sessions after losing custody of her baby girl; a miscarriage of her second child, the result of being thrown down a flight of stairs by her second husband when she was twenty-nine. Janine shook her head, wondering, as she had many times since she'd met Bonnie last summer, how her friend could retain such a near-saintly attitude in the face of such heart-wrenching disappointment.

"I'll tell you something, Bonnie, if that woman said that to me, I don't care if she was having the absolute worst day of her life, I still would've snapped at her."

Bonnie smiled as she watched Janine curl some pad Thai noodles around her plastic fork and pop them into her mouth. Forty-two and older than Bonnie by nine years, Janine was like an older, protective sister. It was a feeling Bonnie enjoyed.

"Well," Bonnie said, watching David and the woman walking back up the makeshift steps of the dumpster. "I'm not saying I wasn't tempted to say something. It's just that there's already so much hostility in the world, I don't want to add to it."

Looking up from her plate, Janine shook her head. "You're far too civilised for our society."

"So, you don't agree then?"

"With what?"

"That there's too much hostility in today's world."

"Oh, I agree with you. As a matter of fact, I couldn't agree with you more," Janine replied, thinking that it required a person to be a practising Buddhist to navigate today's society without wanting to lash out at someone on a near hourly basis. And then, recalling her encounter with a gentleman outside Union Station two weeks ago, how the escalating argument had required the intervention of a nearby police officer, she added, "Unfortunately, unlike yourself, I'm not one for turning the other cheek."

Bonnie smiled at Janine's religious reference, her attention momentarily diverted by a seagull landing on the edge of the dumpster. "Why do you suppose we're like this?" she asked after David had shooed away the bird.

"Like what?"

"The way we are? Always in each other's faces, ready to argue at the drop of a hat."

"You know, a better question might be, why are you like this?"

"Like what?"

"The way you are. Always turning the other cheek, ready to help someone without being asked. I mean, you're not religious. You've had the worst life of anyone I've ever known, and yet, despite all this, you still manage to be so . . . civil."

"Well, I suppose, if I had to guess, I'd say it's because I'm —"

Bonnie's response was interrupted by the sound of a police siren getting closer. Much closer. A moment later David stuck his head into the dumpster.

"Everybody out!" he shouted. "Cops!"

"Let's go!" Janine said, quickly stuffing some food in her handbag before exiting the 'establishment.'

"Oh my God. Did you see that?"

. . . . To Be Continued . . .

I kinda changed my mind . . . .

Keli slid her right hand off the steering wheel and pointed in the direction of the police cruiser that had just veered into an alleyway.

"What?" Tim asked.

"Those people climbing out of that dumpster. There must have been five or six of them."

Bryan chuckled. "They were probably just having dinner."

"I think I'm going to puke."

"Oh, come on, it's not that bad," Bryan said.

"Not that bad? Are you insane? It's revolting."

Bryan shrugged. "Garbage is our greatest natural resource," he said, causing Tim to smile and nod.

Keli despised Bryan. He was always filling Tim's head with his juvenile ideas, trying to convince him to do the things he thought they should be doing (helping the homeless, going tree planting in BC, joining Youth Challenge International), the places he thought they should be visiting (Thailand, Hornby Island, Costa Rica), and the things they should avoid at all costs (settling down, buying a condo, Keli). These ideas were the opposite of what Keli wanted for her and Tim. She wanted her and Tim to get their own place, preferably a condo, right here in Toronto as soon as possible so they could start building a life together. A life that, hopefully, didn't include Bryan.

"You wouldn't believe the kind of food people throw out," Bryan was now saying. "It's completely edible."

"How would *you* know?" Keli asked. "Have you ever eaten out of a dumpster?"

Bryan nodded. "Tons of times. I used to rummage through the dumpsters all the time when Tim and I lived in Kingston."

"I hope you realise how gross and disgusting you are."

"Hey, I wasn't the only one doing it," Bryan said, nudging Tim on the shoulder.

"You?" Keli asked, pointing at Tim.

Tim nodded.

"Oh my God. Do I even know you?"

"There's lots of things you don't know about us," Bryan said, smiling suggestively at Tim.

Keli glared at Bryan. "There's obviously a lot of things I don't *want* to know," she replied. Then, glancing at Tim, she said, "Promise me right now this is something you will never admit to doing."

"I will do no such thing," Bryan said.

"I wasn't talking to you," Keli said, flicking her hand in Bryan's direction like he was a pesky fly before nudging Tim. "Well?"

"I'll see what I can do," Tim replied, sighing.

Tim was tired of the incessant bickering that inevitably occurred whenever Bryan and Keli were together. He wished they could just get along. Of course, he knew this would likely never happen. They had different agendas. Much different.

"What were we talking about before?" Tim asked, trying to steer the conversation away from what they'd been discussing.

"Before what?" Keli asked.

"Before we saw the cops chasing those people out of the dumpster."

"Oh. Um . . . I think I was saying I don't know what to get Ainsley for her birthday."

"Why?"

"Because the woman already has everything. I mean, *everything*."

"Then don't get her *anything*," Bryan said.

"Yeah, right. She'd have a coronary."

"Why?"

"Bryan, you don't just show up to Ainsley Cadeau's birthday bash without a gift."

"Why not?"

"You just don't."

"But you just finished saying she already has everything?"

"So, she'd still want something. She'd be really upset if I didn't bring her something. I mean, she's the type of person who gets upset even when every single person she invites to her party brings her something. But she'd definitely be more upset if I didn't bring her anything."

"That makes absolutely no sense."

"Sure it does," Tim said, smiling. "Want in the midst of plenty."

"Hey, you're right," Bryan said, nodding his head appreciatively at Tim. "You're totally right."

"Excuse me. Did I just miss something?"

"'Want in the midst of plenty,'" Bryan said, obviously delighted that Keli had no clue as to what Tim was talking about. "It's something Alexis de Tocqueville said a long time ago. He was referring to how even when people have plenty of things they still aren't satisfied."

"It's only because they have the wrong kind of plenty," Tim said.

"Exactly," Bryan nodded.

"The wrong kind of plenty?" Keli said, still looking confused.

"Come on, Keli. It's pretty basic stuff," Bryan said, smiling at her when she gave him the finger. "Take your friend, Ainsley, for example. Even though she already has plenty of things, she still wants more. But it doesn't even really matter to her if she gets them or doesn't get them because she's going to be upset anyway. And the reason she's upset is because these things don't fulfill her. They're the wrong kind of plenty. And the more she has, the more they remind her of this fact."

"Was that explanation supposed to make sense to anyone?"

Bryan shrugged. "Anyone with an I.Q. over fifty."

"Oh my *God*. That was, like, *so* hilarious," Keli said, slapping the steering wheel. "You should really consider getting into comedy, Bryan."

"I'll give it some thought. Who knows, maybe when Tim and I are driving out to Van next week, I'll check out the comedy clubs on the way."

"What are you talking about?"

"Oh, I'm sorry," Bryan said, trying his best to stifle a smile. "I guess Tim hasn't told you yet, huh?"

"Told me what yet? Tim?"

Tim hesitated for a few moments. "Um, yeah. Well, I think I'm going to turn down the job here in Toronto."

"What? Why?"

Tim sighed. "I don't know. I guess I'm just not really all that into it right now."

"I thought you said you were?"

"I know, but . . . I don't know. I guess I kinda changed my mind."

Keli shook her head. She couldn't believe what she was hearing. She knew she shouldn't have let the two of them go out alone last night. "Well, what's this about Vancouver? You're not serious are you?"

Tim shrugged. "I don't know. I could sure use the change of scenery. Plus, I really miss the west coast."

"The west is the best," Bryan said, grinning foolishly.

Keli glared at Bryan in the rear-view mirror. He blew her a kiss.

"You're welcome to come along," Tim said. "I mean, I want you to come."

Bryan smiled. He knew Keli wouldn't come. He knew she wanted to settle down. In Toronto. She'd already followed Tim halfway across the country in hopes of getting him to commit to one postal code. And her. But as long as he was around, Bryan wasn't going to allow it. He wasn't going to see his friend marry this conniving little —

"Watch out!"

. . . . To Be Continued . . .

I love that you love her

At the last possible instant, Sandra steered her Saturn station wagon safely out of the path of the car cutting in front of her before quickly returning to her lane.

"What an idiot!" Ted shouted, his right hand still squeezing the passenger side door handle. "No signal, no warning, just — Wham! I'm going to turn right in front of you and cut you off."

"I can't believe I didn't hit them," Sandra said.

Ted reached over and massaged her neck. "You were amazing, hon," he said. "Great reaction."

"Thanks," Sandra replied, smiling. She took a deep breath and shook her head. "Whew! I can feel my heart pounding in my chest."

"Mine, too. I guess it's a good thing the old man wasn't still in the car. He probably would've had another heart attack."

Sandra chuckled. Ted's father had just spent three days with them. He was part of a nationwide study tracking the health of patients who'd had heart surgery and was getting some follow-up tests done. She and Ted had just dropped him off at the train station and were on their way back home.

"I was serious, you know," Sandra said a few moments later.

"About what?"

"When I said I thought it was remarkable you were able to endure so much abuse and come out of it unscathed."

Sandra was referring to the conversation she and Ted were having before being cut off by the car. They'd been discussing Ted's upbringing, specifically how Ted's father had carried on the family tradition of the man of the house taking his frustration out on the eldest son using various methods — hands, fists, belts, a wooden cane.

"I guess," Ted said, as Sandra pulled the station wagon into their driveway. "The strange part about him was he could be the warmest, most compassionate man I knew and then, the next moment, the cruelest. It was pretty confusing."

"Well, thankfully, it wasn't transferred to you."

Ted smiled, was about to say, "I just take it out on Muffin," then reconsidered, thinking Sandra wouldn't think that was funny. "I guess I'll see you in a couple of hours then?"

Sandra nodded. "I shouldn't be any longer."

"Okay, I'll see —"

"Oh, look at Muffin," Sandra said, suddenly, pointing through the windshield at their Chesapeake Bay retriever, clearly visible through the front bay window of their duplex. "Look at her tail."

Ted smiled as he watched Muffin's tail whirling round and round like a helicopter blade. "Hopefully she'll like these treats," he said, tapping the bag of cheese-and-bacon–flavoured doggy treats they'd picked up at the pet store after dropping off his father.

"I still don't know why she doesn't like the other ones," Sandra said. "She used to love them."

Ted shrugged. "She probably just likes a little variety."

"Yeah, well, personally, I think she's being a suck. And you've got to stop spoiling her with all these new foods. We must have at least a dozen half-eaten bags of dog food and treats laying around the house by now. It's getting to be expensive."

"Ah, she's worth it," Ted said. "She's a great dog."

Sandra smiled and pulled Ted towards her, kissing him. "I have to admit, I love that you love her."

"Hey, she's our baby girl, right? How could I not love her?"

They had purchased her two years ago, when Muffin was only six weeks old. Ted had done hours of research on the Internet, talked with dozens of dog owners, and visited a whole slew of breeders before finally deciding on a Chesapeake Bay retriever. Then they went to three different Chesapeake Bay breeders before choosing Muffin.

"Well, I'll see you in a couple of hours," Ted said, leaning over and giving Sandra another kiss before getting out of the station wagon and walking up the driveway.

After opening the screen door and unlocking the main door, he turned to wave at Sandra as she drove away, remaining in the doorway until the station wagon was out of sight before quickly stepping inside the house, locking the screen door, and dead-bolting the main door.

"Muffin! Here, girl," Ted said, tossing his wallet on the counter as he walked into the kitchen. "Where are you, girl?"

A moment or two later he spotted her. She was in the living room, curled up in her basket, the one Sandra bought for her the day they brought her home from the breeder. Inside the basket, positioned next to her snout, was a pair of Sandra's slippers. Ted's slippers were still in their usual spot, tucked under the avonne bench in the hallway.

"There you are," Ted said, smiling and walking over to her.

Lately, he'd noticed Muffin wasn't nearly as happy to see him as she used to be. She used to bark and dance, nuzzle his leg, and nip at his trousers the moment he came through the door. Now, if he wasn't accompanied by Sandra, Muffin would immediately retreat to the refuge of her basket.

Crouching down beside Muffin, Ted snatched Sandra's slippers out of the basket and tossed them in the direction of the avonne bench.

"Well, even though you don't like me that much any more," Ted said in a soothing voice, beginning to pet Muffin's sulking head. "I still went out and bought you something."

When Ted opened the bag of treats, Muffin immediately raised her head out of the basket and began sniffing the cheese-and-bacon–scented air. Her tail started wagging. Ted pulled a biscuit from the bag, placed it in his hand, and held it out for Muffin. Moving her head slightly forward, Muffin tentatively took the treat in her mouth and was about to start chewing it when Ted slapped her, swift and hard, across the snout, causing her to yelp — and the biscuit, slightly slimy, but still intact, to pop out of her mouth.

Ted picked it up and held it out for her again. This time Muffin didn't take it. "Not hungry, girl?" he asked, calmly.

Ted waited a few more moments and then placed the treat in the basket beside Muffin before walking into the kitchen. After making himself a snack, he was about to go into the study when he noticed Muffin hadn't yet eaten the treat.

"Your mommy was really hoping you'd like this brand," Ted said, picking up the biscuit and offering it to her. Muffin turned her head away from it. Ted noticed she was panting. "It's okay, girl. It's okay," he said gently, petting Muffin a few times before beginning to force the biscuit into her mouth by prying open her jaw and cramming it between the gaps in her teeth until it was sitting on her tongue.

"*Bon appetit*," he said on his way to the bathroom to retrieve a hand mirror. Returning a few moments later, he saw that Muffin had already spat out the biscuit.

"Tsk, tsk, tsk," Ted said, waving a disapproving finger at Muffin. "Where are your manners, girl?"

Once again Ted picked up the now slightly mangled, mucous-covered biscuit and stuffed it back into Muffin's mouth before walking around the corner and, using the hand mirror, watching Muffin eventually spit it out. Ted stuffed it back into Muffin's mouth, and in an effort to get Muffin to swallow the biscuit, clamped her mouth shut tight with his right hand and placed his left over her snout, cutting off her air supply. As Muffin tried frantically to pull away, Ted talked to her in soothing tones, telling her she was a good girl, his hand remaining tightly cupped around her snout until she started sucking air in through her mouth, causing her to choke on the biscuit.

For the past few months, whenever Sandra wasn't home, Ted had been doing this to Muffin — the entire time talking nicely to her, affecting a pleasant, cheery, sometimes compassionate tone of voice that he knew, given his actions, confused the hell out of Muffin.

It was the same technique Ted's father had employed when he was about to start beating Ted. He would speak to him without raising his voice, using an amiable, affectionate tone, as though he was actually pleased with Ted.

"Do you realise how many starving dogs there are in the world who would beg for this kind of treat?" Ted was now saying to Muffin, letting go of her snout and cuffing her, causing her to yelp and jump out of the basket.

Ted and Sandra hadn't had children. In fact, Ted had gone out of his way to find someone who didn't want children, being every bit as thorough in his research and selection of Sandra as he had been with Muffin. The truth was, he was afraid to have kids. He thought he'd turn against them, do to them what his father had done to him. He had no idea this sort of thing could be transferred to a dog. And, at least for a while, it looked like it wouldn't be.

From the moment he chose her, he gave Muffin an inordinate amount of affection, love, and attention — to the point that Sandra frequently commented on it, jokingly referring to Muffin as Ted's "baby girl." Then, a little over a year ago, Ted noticed a shift occurred in his feelings towards Muffin. Initially almost imperceptible, the shift became more pronounced with each passing week. He didn't know why, but little things about Muffin began to bother him: having to clean up after her; that she sometimes knocked things over or left hairs on their expensive carpets and area rugs; that she barked whenever the doorbell rang or she heard another dog walking along the sidewalk.

Ted was now watching Muffin slinking around the living room, her head down, body low to the floor, tail between her legs, undoubtedly trying to decide whether upstairs or downstairs would provide her with the most sanctuary. Ted hoped she'd choose downstairs. There was less chance of the neighbours hearing anything.

Muffin turned to go upstairs.

"Stay!" Ted shouted.

Muffin froze.

Ted walked up to her and screamed in her left ear, a maniacal, blood-curdling scream that caused Muffin to abruptly turn and run, her claws frantically scratching at the smooth marble tile flooring, desperately trying to find some purchase as she scampered towards the basement door.

Ted followed. "Muffin. Here, Muffin," he called after her as he descended the spiral staircase leading to the basement, rage growing inside him with each step.

He found her cowering in the corner of the recreation room behind the Ikea sofa chair. Bending down on one knee, he pushed the sofa chair away from the wall. "Come on, Muffin. Here, girl," he said, trying to coax her out of her hiding spot.

Reluctantly, Muffin moved her left paw forward a few inches.

"That's a good girl," Ted said, gently. "Come on, come on."

Muffin nudged her right paw forward slightly, then withdrew it.

"Muffin!" Ted shouted. "Come here!"

Muffin backed away from Ted, shoving herself into the corner. Smiling serenely, Ted got up, walked behind the bar, and retrieved a hand-carved wooden cane, the one he received for his fortieth birthday two years ago as a joke from his father-in-law. After a few practice swings, he walked back to the sofa chair. Muffin was almost hyperventilating now, her legs shaking uncontrollably. While positioning the chair in such a way as to trap Muffin in the corner, Ted saw the tiny puddle between her legs. She'd urinated on the floor.

Feeling an uncontrollable malevolence moving through him, Ted tapped the steel tip of the cane twice on the basement floor and then slowly lifted it. Muffin, her eyes firmly focussed on the rising cane, began to whimper. Ted called her a good girl, twice, doing his best to remove the violence from his voice. Despite this, Muffin continued to whimper, her eyes alternating quickly between Ted and the cane now suspended high above Ted's head until — the instant he called her a good girl for the third time — she suddenly perked up her ears and began barking, loudly.

En route to the front door, Ted took a few moments to compose himself, inspecting his appearance in the hallway mirror. He couldn't believe how much he now looked like his father did when he was Ted's age — same dishevelled hair, same red cheeks, same eyes clouded with madness.

Unlocking the front door, Ted opened it and saw an attractive brunette standing on his front step.

"Hi," she said. "Are you, by any chance, Ralph Davidson?"

Ted unlocked the screen door and opened it. "Nope," he said, poking his head outside. "He lives just down the way. House number 132. This is 123."

"Oh," the woman said, looking slightly confused. She reached into her purse and pulled out a card. "Oh, you're right. My mistake," she said, pointing at the house number beside Ted's door. "I must be dyslexic. Sorry to bother you."

"No bother at all. Glad I could help."

For a moment Ted thought about asking her what she wanted with Ralph. He and Ralph had been very neighbourly until Ralph witnessed Ted disciplining Muffin after she'd knocked Ted's wine glass off the arm of his Muskoka chair. "Say hi to Ralph for me, will you?"

. . . . To Be Continued . . .

to be continued . . . .

"I will," Geena said, smiling at the man before walking down the front steps, slightly disappointed that he was wearing a wedding ring. When she reached the last step, she suddenly stopped. "Who shall I say said 'Hi'?" she asked, turning around.

"Ted."

"Okay. Thanks again."

Geena continued up the street to house number 132, thinking about Ted, why he was sweating, wondering what she had interrupted. A minute later, while staring at the front bay window of Ted's house, a short man with a comb-over answered the door she'd just knocked on.

"Hi," he said. "Geena?"

Geena nodded. "Ralph?"

"That's me."

They shook hands.

"Come on in," Ralph said, gesturing for Geena to step inside.

"Sorry I'm late. I mixed up the house number."

"Not a worry. We're still waiting for another member to show up, anyway."

"Oh, by the way, Ted, the man at the house I went to, said to say 'Hi' to you."

Ralph smiled. "He did, did he?"

Geena nodded. "Is he a friend of yours?"

"Friend? No, not really."

"Does he attend these meetings?"

Ralph shook his head. "Ted? No. Ted has, well, let's just say Ted has other interests. And issues."

"Oh."

After telling Geena she could keep her shoes on, Ralph led her into a sizeable living room equipped with a large elbow couch, two love seats, three La-Z-Boy chairs, and several wooden chairs. Most of the available seating space was already occupied by the dozen or so persons in attendance. Several bowls of chips and pretzels, three kinds of no-name pop, a tower of plastic cups, and an ice bucket had been set out on a card table positioned in one corner of the room. In the opposite corner, a large TV had been completely hollowed out and was now, with the help of a few fitted shelves, home to a couple dozen books, a house plant, and several unlit votive candles.

"Everyone," Ralph said, escorting Geena to the centre of the room, "this is Geena. It's her first meeting."

"Hello, Geena," everyone replied, smiling warmly.

After shaking hands with a few of the members, including Ralph's wife, Geena took a moment to assess the men in the room. A few months ago, Geena told a friend that thanks to her daughter Kimberley successfully sabotaging every potential relationship she'd had in the last year, she desperately needed to expand her opportunities to meet men. Her friend had told her about a recent trend in meeting people at "special interest" group gatherings. 'There are literally hundreds of them in the GTA, with plenty of eligible men,' her friend had said. 'You just have to be willing to do a little legwork.' Apparently her friend had met her now fiancé at the High Park chapter of this very group. Scouring the room again to confirm that all of the men present were either wearing a wedding band or were far too rumpled and unrefined for her tastes, Geena sighed, doubting she would have the same luck as her friend. Oh well, she thought, glancing at her watch. The night is still young. Drew's at her sleepover and Kimberley won't be back until midnight. I suppose I could always excuse myself early and hit a —

"The meeting will start as soon as Kenneth arrives," Ralph called out. "Or, in five minutes, whichever comes first."

"So our legendary couch potato is late again, huh?" a middle-aged man wearing a linen suit and a neatly trimmed goatee said, coming up from behind Ralph and Geena. "He probably didn't want to miss his favourite cooking show."

Well, well, well, Geena said to herself. What have we here?

"Hi, there," Matt said, extending his hand towards Geena. "I don't believe we've met. My name's Matt."

"Geena," she said, shaking Matt's hand a little longer than was necessary under the circumstances.

"Nice to meet you, Geena. Is this your first meeting?"

Geena nodded. "And you?"

Matt shook his head. "I've been TV-free for more than a dozen years now."

"Braggart," blurted a woman seated on the end of the elbow couch.

Matt turned and smiled at the woman. "It's not bragging if it's true."

Geena took the momentary distraction provided by the woman's comment to continue her appraisal of Matt: no wedding ring (and no sign of a wedding ring having recently inhabited the space); semi-expensive looking suit; taller than her by three, maybe four inches (and she was in heels); passable selection of dress shoes; nearly full head of hair; nice teeth, great smile. The only thing she could find fault with so far was the goatee. If they made it past the first few dates, it would have to go. Drew and Kimberley hated goatees on men over the age of twenty-one.

"You're not serious, are you?" Geena said, trying to make it sound like this was the most incredulous and wonderful thing she'd ever heard. "You've really been TV-free for all that time?"

Matt nodded.

"That's amazing."

"Thank you."

"How did you do it?"

"I quit. Cold turkey."

198

"Really? You mean you never went back?"

"Never."

"Not even once?"

"Not even once."

"That's remarkable."

"Matt's an exceptional case," Ralph said at this point. "And trust me, we don't expect or demand a completely TV-free lifestyle from our members. We hope for it, but it's not our main objective. Our goal is temperance. Moderation."

"So, why'd you stop watching?" Geena said, shifting her position slightly, angling her body in an attempt to close Ralph off from any further intrusion into the discussion she was having with Matt.

"I stopped watching the moment I found out they cancelled the show, *My So-Called Life*."

"I love that show," Geena said. "Claire Danes and Jared Leto were in it, right?"

"That's the one."

Geena had purchased the DVD set a few years ago, adding it to her sizeable collection. The younger sister in the show used to remind her of Kimberley. Now, Kimberly was more like a bitchier version of Claire Danes' character. "So, you stopped watching because they cancelled the show?"

Matt nodded. "It was one of the few shows at the time that actually made you think, that depicted real people dealing with real issues. I couldn't get over the fact that a show as real and gritty as *My So-Called Life* was cancelled after only one year when some stupid, saccharine show like *Beverly Hills, 90210* stayed on the air forever."

"And you swear you haven't watched TV since?" Geena asked.

Matt shook his head. "Not even for a few seconds."

"Don't you miss it?"

"What's there to miss?"

"You're kidding, right?" Geena said, giving Matt a look as though she were waiting for him to start nodding his head. "Some of the shows nowadays are really amazing. And with all the specialty channels available on cable and satellite you can pretty much watch anything you want. You should really check it out some —"

Geena stopped talking, suddenly realising several of the other members were now staring at her, regarding her as though she was a lobbyist for the TV industry. Curb your enthusiasm, Geena, my dear, she told herself, smiling sheepishly at the other members. They don't know you're not here to give up TV. Oh, God, as if I could do that. It's the only time Kimberley can actually stand to sit in the same room with me longer than a few seconds.

"So, I take it you're still quite . . . *attached* to your TV," Matt said.

Geena bowed her head slightly and nodded. "But, I'm seriously considering filing for a divorce," she replied, smiling.

Matt chuckled, half-heartedly. So much for him, Geena thought. Perhaps this Kenneth person will be different. Perhaps he won't be such a bloody bore.

"Okay, everyone. It doesn't look like Kenneth will be joining us tonight," Ralph said, pointing at his watch. "Perhaps we can all take a seat. And since we have a few new members joining us today, maybe we should go around the room, say who we are, and why we're here."

After waiting until everyone was seated, Ralph turned to his left and, gesturing to a man seated on one of the wooden chairs, said, "Would you like to start us off, Sid?"

"Sure. Hello, everyone. For those of you who don't know me, my name is Sidney and I've been watching TV since I can remember. When I was a kid I watched shows like *Sesame Street*, *Polka Dot Door*, *Mr. Dress-up*, *Bugs Bunny*. And the older I got, the more I watched. It eventually got to the point where my entire day was planned around watching TV. I even married a fellow TV-junkie just so I wouldn't have to deal with someone pestering me to go for a hike or a bike ride. We had the full cable package and two satellite dishes. We had three VCRs in the house and we taped all the shows we couldn't watch. Our basement was packed with hundreds of VHS tapes. Hundreds. We had episodes of shows dating back ten years ago that we still hadn't watched. I didn't admit I had a problem until I was at my nephew's baptism. Just as the priest was asking for the nephew's godparents to come forward, I realised I'd forgotten to set my VCR and I bolted out of the church. Can you believe that? I was supposed to be my nephew's godfather. I walked out on his baptism because I didn't want to miss *Magnum P.I.* That's why I'm here."

"Thank you, Sidney. Who's next?"

"That would be me. Hello everyone. My name is Linda. I guess the reason I'm here is largely in part because my husband has destroyed our big screen TV four times now — and it's ruining our marriage. We've spent over ten thousand dollars on televisions in six years. All the money we've spent on getting new TVs was supposed to go towards us taking a really nice vacation, something we haven't done since we went on our honeymoon seven years ago."

"Excuse me," Matt said, putting up his hand. "If you don't mind my asking, why does your husband always wreck the TV?"

"He's really into sports. He loves baseball and hockey and when his team doesn't win or they play poorly, he gets upset and throws things at it. Usually a beer bottle. Three weeks ago, after he threw a baseball at it, I finally told him that I'd had it. I wasn't going to put up with a stupid TV keeping us from going on vacation. I told him he had a choice to make. I said, 'One of us has to go — either me or the TV.'"

"What happened?" Matt asked.

"Well, I'm living at my sister's right now and he's at our place watching football on his new big-screen TV."

Matt shook his head. "Some people."

"Okay, now," Ralph said. "Remember, let's reserve judgement. Are you finished, Linda? Okay. Thank you. Who's next? Molly?"

"Hello everyone, my name is Molly and I've been a TV addict for most of the nineteen years I've been alive. I guess I partly blame my parents for my addiction since the entire time I was growing up there was a TV on in the house. It was what we did as a family. We didn't go on family outings to the science centre or the art gallery or the museum or the zoo or a park or even to Canada's Wonderland. We watched TV. It wasn't until recently that I realised how isolated and removed we were from the real world. I wanted us to actually go out and do something instead of watching other people do it for us on TV. Of course, as soon as I mentioned this to my parents, my father said something like, 'Isolated from reality? What are you talking about? What about all the reality TV shows we watch?'"

A few members nodded their heads and chuckled.

"As far as I can tell," Matt interrupted, "the term 'reality show' is every bit as much of an oxymoron as 'military intelligence' or 'friendly fire.' Think about it. Anyone with half a neuron in their brain knows that if you have a dozen cameras poking in your face, you're not going to behave in the same manner as if there was no one else around. Not to mention that all these shows from what I hear are scripted, directed, edited, and produced by slick TV industry professionals. How can anyone in their right mind call this reality?"

A few members shrugged.

"I'll bet you none of these shows are anywhere near as good or as interesting or as real or as potentially life-altering as a thirty-minute walk down Yonge Street."

"Amen," Ralph said. "Okay, people. I believe Dave is next."

"Hello, everyone. My name is Dave and I relapsed yesterday. I watched TV for almost eighteen hours. I couldn't shut it off. I'm sorry."

"No need to apologise, Dave," Ralph said. "Remember, we're not expecting miracles. You'll do better today." Then, turning and smiling at Barry, he said, "I believe you're up."

"Hi, my name is Barry and I'm here to try and find some alternatives to TV. My three boys are addicted to it. If they're not watching it, they're playing video games on it. I don't think it's healthy but so far, my wife Patty and I haven't been able to find something to replace it."

Ralph nodded his head. "It's an unfortunate but familiar situation. The good thing is, there are lots of people here today who have gone through what you're going through. And they can suggest alternative activities."

"Like what?"

"Well, for instance, our family plays this storytelling sequencing game called To Be Continued where — oh, excuse me, everyone," Ralph said, suddenly springing up from his seat in response to the ringing doorbell. "That's probably just Kenneth."

The other members turned to watch Ralph as he made his way to the front door, opening it and bowing as though he were greeting royalty.

"Help! Please help! My husband just collapsed. He's on the side-walk! Please someone. Help him!"

The woman, probably in her sixties, tears streaming down her face, lips quivering uncontrollably, was standing with her hands together, as though she were praying, frantically looking at the people gathered in Ralph's living room, waiting for one of them to move.

Glancing over the woman's shoulder, Ralph saw the unmoving, prostrate body on the sidewalk. "I'll call 911," he said, pointing towards the phone in the hall. "Does anyone here know CPR?" he shouted at the group.

Geena knew CPR. She'd been re-certified two months ago as part of her job. She also knew that as soon as she started to perform CPR on this woman's husband she would have to continue — "To the best of her ability" — until the paramedics arrived or someone else who knew CPR took over. It was the unwritten rule of First Aid. Geena wondered how many other people in the room knew CPR but weren't admitting it. Hadn't that guy over there, what's his name — Barry? Hadn't she overheard him saying he was a surgeon?

"Please! Someone! Help!" the woman screamed, hysterically, running out the front door.

Geena abruptly jumped up from her seat and ran after the woman. As soon as she got outside, however, she saw that the woman's husband was already being attended to by a young man. Geena sighed. This had always been her problem. Waiting for someone else to make a decision. To take action. It was the reason she hadn't divorced her husband ten years ago, waiting instead for him to make the decision to end things.

Other group members were now brushing past her, hurrying to

join the people already encircling the fallen man. Somewhere, in the distance, Geena heard an ambulance siren getting closer.

"Can anyone take over for me here?"

The question startled Geena. "I can," she replied, quickly, without thinking, feeling thankful for the second chance.

"Do you know what you're doing?" the young man performing CPR asked.

Geena nodded. She eased herself into position and took over.

"Thanks a lot," the young man said, standing up and starting to back away, moving into the street. "I'll go and get a blanket from my —"

The bleat of a car horn cut the young man's sentence short.

. . . . **To Be Continued . . .**

and he doesn't have a clue? . . . . . .

"What is it with people today?" Lauren said, shaking her head. "First some crazy chick walks over my car. And now this guy."

"Just another day of driving in Toronto," Dennis replied, throwing a glance over his shoulder at the guy running to his parked car.

"I think I'm starting to regret doing this for you."

"Hey, I really appreciate it, Lauren. Trust me."

"I'm just kidding. By the way, just so I'm clear, I'm with you because . . . ?"

"Because you're my out. If I did this alone I'd end up having to stay all evening listening to my grandfather blab on about something stupid. This way I'll just tell him I have to go because we've got something to do. Plus, you're going to tell him what a great guy I am."

Lauren smiled. "How much am I charging you for this again?"

"Whatever you like. Oh, yeah. Did I mention my grandfather has a soft spot for young, attractive women with auburn hair?"

"Not until now."

"Well, he does."

"Well, what about dyed auburn hair? You know this isn't my real colour."

"He'll never notice."

Lauren smiled. "It's nice to know I'm being used. So, what would you like me to say on your behalf?"

Dennis shrugged. "I don't know. Just make sure it's nice."

"You want me to lie, then?" Lauren said.

"Very funny."

"Alright, I think I can come up with a few things to say."

"Such as?"

"Such as, 'Dennis is a wonderful, handsome, hard-working, and loving grandson who has nothing but good things to say about his equally wonderful and handsome grandfather.'"

"Well, that might be laying it on a little thick. But, then again, coming from you, he might actually believe it."

"Out of the mouths of young, attractive women with auburn hair comes . . ."

"Exactly. Well, here we are. This is it," Dennis said, pointing to the next driveway.

"Holy shit! You weren't kidding. He *is* rich," Lauren said as she pulled her car into the gated driveway, taking in the near-palatial home. "This place must be worth a fortune."

Dennis nodded. "It is. Now, just remember. We're going to keep it short and sweet. Ten, maybe twenty, minutes. Maximum. I'll give him the book. We'll chat for a bit. You can tell him how great I am. And then we'll make up some excuse why we have to go."

"Like what?"

Dennis shrugged. "I don't know. We'll tell him we've got tickets to see a movie. Sound good?"

"Sure. Tickets for a movie. Got it."

"And be firm. He'll probably try to get us to stay longer."

"Why?"

"He just will. I know my grandfather. And he can be pretty persuasive. So be firm, okay?"

"I'll do my best."

A few moments after Dennis had rung the doorbell, some coughing and grumbling could be heard on the other side of the large, formidable front door. When it opened, an elderly man, of elegant appearance and in relatively good shape, stepped into the doorway.

"Hi, Grandpa," Dennis said, trying to sound cheerful, offering him his hand. "How are you?"

"Fine. Just fine," his grandfather replied, ignoring Dennis's outstretched hand, choosing, instead, to focus his attention on Lauren. "Who's this?"

"This, Grandpa," Dennis replied, smiling and stepping slightly aside, "is Lauren. Lauren, this is my grandfather, Mr. Henri Easton."

"*Enchantée, mademoiselle,*" Henri said, offering Lauren his hand.

"*À vous de même, Monsieur,*" Lauren replied, accepting Henri's hand.

"*Vous parlez français?*" Henri said, obviously delighted.

"*Mais bien sûr, Monsieur.*"

"You should teach this one," Henri said, throwing his thumb in Dennis's direction. "Tell me again why you don't speak French?" he said, casting a disparaging glance at Dennis.

"Um, I don't know," Dennis said, shrugging.

Henri shook his head. "Always the same answer. I ask a simple question and he shrugs his shoulders and mumbles, 'I don't know' or some equally inane response."

When Lauren chuckled Dennis frowned at her. Laughing at him did not fall under the auspices of 'putting in a good word for him.'

"Well, come on in," Henri said, nudging Dennis to the side to allow Lauren to pass first into the front foyer.

"Thank you," Lauren replied, taking Henri's hand and stepping inside Henri's regal and recently renovated Victorian-style home.

For nearly a century now the Easton's majestic mansion — along with its impeccably manicured grounds — had been the *pièce de resistance* of the Rosedale neighbourhood, a stately structure presiding over the surrounding homes and estates, occasionally directing a disapproving frown at a neighbour's decision to modernise traditional façades and landscape designs.

"You're down to thirty-seven dollars in your book account, Grandpa," Dennis said, handing Henri the book he'd requested.

"Yes, yes. I'm sure I'll be fine for a while," Henri replied, taking the opportunity, with Lauren's back now turned to him, to evaluate her from behind.

Dennis smiled, silently congratulating himself on his idea to have Lauren accompany him.

"Wow, this is beautiful," Lauren said, lightly brushing the sleek mahogany deacon's bench stationed near the front door with her fingertips. "Is this a, um, what do you call it again?"

"It's a Ukranian-style deacon's bench," Dennis replied. "The original design dates back to the early nineteenth century. Last year we had a marble Rousseau bench there. And the year before that a —"

Dennis felt his grandfather's hand on his shoulder and stopped talking.

"So, my dear," Henri said, a moment later, gently placing his arm around Lauren's shoulder and guiding her into the receiving room. "Where did you learn to speak French?"

"Martinique."

"Martinique? What a magnificent island."

"You've been?"

Henri nodded. "Many times. How long were you there?"

"The first time for a week. The second time I stayed for a month."

"One month? *C'est magnifique.* I keep telling my grandson here that he should take time off and go somewhere exotic, but he never does."

"That's what I tell him, too," Lauren said, smiling. "But he insists that spending time with you is more important than taking a vacation."

Henri raised an eyebrow and inclined his head in Dennis's direction, gazing at him as though he were wondering why he was still here. "There's something that requires your attention in the guest bathroom," he said after a moment, pausing before opening the double French doors leading into the living room.

"Which one?"

"The second one."

"Another surprise?"

"More of an accident, really. You'll find all you need beneath the vanity."

"You want to come and —"

"No, no, no. She's fine with me here. I'll entertain her in your absence," Henri said, showing Lauren into the living room.

Dennis shook his head, mouthed something to Lauren about putting in a good word, and walked to the second guest room. Five minutes later he had rejoined Lauren and his grandfather in the living room.

"That was quite the accident, Grandpa."

Henri, in the process of describing what had prompted him to purchase this particular Tom Thomson painting, waved his hand dismissively at Dennis. "Don't make such a big deal about it, boy. It's not as though you went into a boardroom and saved me from insolvency. You just cleaned up some poop."

Grimacing, Dennis shoved his fists deep into the front pockets of his trousers. He wanted desperately to tell his grandfather to go to hell. Better yet, he wanted to retrieve the feces he'd scooped off the heated marble-tiled floor in the second guest bathroom and smear it all over his grandfather's precious Tom Thomson painting.

"So, what have you two been talking about?" Dennis asked instead, looking at Lauren, waiting for her to wink or nod or give him some indication that she'd put in a good word for him.

"Dinner," his grandfather said. "Are you hungry?"

"Not really," Dennis replied.

"Just as I suspected," Henri said, placing his hand on Lauren's forearm. "You see, I know my grandson very well."

"Yes, you do."

"So, then. It seems it will be just the two of us. I'm certain Dennis can find something else to do with his time while we're eating."

"What are you talking about?"

"Your grandfather just ordered dinner for us," Lauren said, shrugging her shoulders and mouthing the words, "I'm sorry."

"It turns out the poor girl is starving," Henri said, regarding Lauren with pity. "And look at the time. She and I are probably the only two people in Toronto who haven't eaten dinner yet."

Clapping his hands together, he began moving in the direction of the nearby frosted glass and stainless steel bar. "Shall we start things off with an aperitif?" Henri said, retrieving two glasses.

"I don't think —"

Henri put up his hand, cutting Dennis off in mid-sentence. "Since you're not eating dinner, Dennis, you will have no need for an aperitif. Besides, I wouldn't want you to be arrested for drinking and driving."

"I didn't drive. Lauren did."

"But you'll be taking her car."

"Excuse me?"

"It's already been arranged."

Dennis removed his hands from his pockets and made a gesture to corroborate his uncomprehending expression.

"Oh, don't stand on ceremony, boy. I already told Pierre you were coming."

"Pierre? You ordered take-out from Pierre? For the two of you?"

"Yes."

"And you want *me* to go and pick it up?"

Henri nodded. "In celebration of my fellow voyager from Martinique," he said, smiling at Lauren.

"But Pierre's restaurant is on the other side of the city. It'll take me half an hour just to get there."

"That is precisely how long Pierre said it would take to prepare the meal," Henri said, glaring at Dennis. And then, turning back to Lauren, he smiled and added, "You see how things work out?"

Dennis shook his head. This was what he was afraid would happen. This was why he insisted he and Lauren stay for only ten, twenty minutes. *Maximum.* This was why he wanted Lauren to tell his grandfather that they had tickets to see a movie. He'd only wanted to tease his grandfather with Lauren's company, so he could use it as leverage for later on.

"We were actually planning on seeing a —"

"Oh, she already told me about that silly movie you were planning to see," Henri said, cutting Dennis off. "A complete waste of time, in my opinion."

"Whatever you say, Grandpa," Dennis said, shaking his head and sighing loudly. "You coming, Lauren?"

"Um. Yeah, well, of course I —"

"Oh, heavens no, my dear. You'll do nothing of the sort," Henri

211

said, waving his hand vigorously in Dennis's direction, as though he was trying to shoo away his grandson's suggestion. "You'll remain here with me. It'll give us time to get acquainted."

"So, what, I'm going by myself?"

"If it's too much trouble I suppose I can call your cousin, Maggie, to pick it up for us. I'm certain she'd be delighted to assist her grandfather."

Dennis sighed. "It's no trouble. I'll see you in an hour or so."

"Don't be late. I don't want the food to be ruined."

Dennis punctuated his grandfather's parting instructions by slamming the front door.

"Now then," Henri said, carrying their drinks over to Lauren while nodding in the direction of the front door, "that's much better, don't you think?"

Lauren stifled a giggle. "You're horrible, Mr. Easton," she said.

"Please, call me Henri," Henri replied, handing Lauren her rye and ginger before taking a sip of his scotch. "And there is good reason for my horribleness. Of that, you can be certain."

Henri had been looking forward to the arrival of his grandson all day, and not just in anticipation of witnessing Dennis's reluctant acquiescence to yet another petty and degrading task, no doubt carried out in hopes of adding a few more items to his inheritance list. Although Henri enjoyed toying with Dennis immensely, wondering just how low his grandson would stoop before he told Henri to go screw himself, the real reason for today's anticipation involved a surprise. And not just any old surprise. This surprise was the culmination of five years of preparation, planning, and execution on Henri's behalf. He couldn't wait to see the expression on his grandson's face when he told him. Of course, when Henri had opened the door a few minutes ago, he was not expecting to find such a treasure on his doorstep.

Like any man of his financial means, he was not unaccustomed to the companionship of beautiful women many years younger than himself. Although he could only be considered mildly attractive, after his wife's death some twenty-five years ago, there had been no shortage of women seeking solace in his ageing arms and burgeoning pocket-book.

Even if it was his desire to try (and it was not), Henri had no delusions that his enormous wealth could erase the more than forty-five years separating he and Lauren. Despite this, he could not prevent himself from admiring her many physical charms.

Though she was perhaps a little too thin in the waist and hips for his tastes, and her breasts, given her relatively small stature, seemed slightly overdeveloped, they were the only minor imperfections he could detect. And, when set against her soft, supple neck, her elegant shoulders, her thick, auburn hair, her creamy skin, and her flawless face, they seemed smaller still.

Watching Lauren sipping her drink while gazing at the Rembrandt opposite the Tom Thomson, he silently applauded his grandson's effort to curry favour. When Henri had intentionally let it slip last week that in his youth he had adored women with auburn hair, stating that he could not resist them as he believed them to be the most intelligent and alluring women in the world, he had no idea Dennis would pick up on this clue, let alone make it happen. Ah, Dennis, my boy, Henri said to himself. You've outdone yourself this time.

"How's your drink, Lauren?"

"Perfect, thank you."

"Shall we sit over here?" Henri said, gesturing towards a large, rigid-looking sectional sofa.

"Sure."

When they were both seated, Henri fixed his gaze firmly on Lauren's hazel eyes. "You're not with him, are you?"

"Who?"

"Dennis."

"What do you mean?"

"Dating. Going steady. In a relationship. Whatever the term is these days."

Lauren shook her head. "No. Why do you ask?"

Henri smiled. "I'm testing your I.Q."

"By asking me if I'm dating your grandson?"

"You can tell a lot about a person by who they date."

Lauren chuckled. "I suppose you're right."

"So, why are you not with him?

"He's not my type."

"And what type might that be?"

Lauren shrugged.

"I hope that shrug isn't going to be accompanied by the words, 'I don't know.'"

Lauren smiled. "After hearing your comment on the subject, I shall refrain."

"Thank you," Henri said, pausing to take a sip of scotch. "Well?"

"Well, I suppose my type has varied over time. If you had asked me that question two years —"

"Pardon me," Henri said, "but would you mind terribly if I attempted to divine this information for myself?"

"Not at all," Lauren said. "Be my guest."

"Excellent," Henri replied, then, after taking another sip of scotch, he returned his gaze to Lauren. "Before I begin, satisfy something for me. The two trips to Martinique; the first was with an ex-boyfriend, yes?"

Lauren smiled. "Ben."

"And the second time you went was shortly after you broke up with Ben and you went with your current beau, correct?"

"Impressive," Lauren replied, nodding her head appreciatively.

"Merely the warm-up, my dear," Henri said, setting his scotch down on the glass end table. "Now, for the main event. If I was a betting man, and I am, I would say that, initially, your type was the proverbial bad boy, the *Rebel Without a Cause* type. Someone who was almost always late in meeting you because he was too busy staring at himself in a mirror, dashing off to a tanning salon, going for rides on his motorcycle, or doing abdominal exercises in a gym. However, your interest in this type changed around the time you and Ben parted ways. You began to find yourself attracted to a man with considerably more depth. He may not have been as good looking or as fit as your previous type, but what he lacked in looks, he made up for in charm. And intelligence. He was the studious type, learned, who regularly patronised bookstores and had a genuine love of literature. Of course, all this depth and study implied a certain seasoning, so I would have to say your new man is older than the previous type. Nothing too dramatic, mind you. Nothing to interest the tabloids. But older, nonetheless."

Henri retrieved his scotch and took a sip. "How did I do?" he asked, barely able to contain his smile.

Lauren laughed. "That's, well . . . I have to say, that's very perceptive."

"Not far off, then?"

"Not at all. In fact, I'm wondering if you've been chatting with Dennis."

"Not to worry. Our relationship is confined to matters of business."

"I see."

"So," Henri said, swirling the ice cubes around his glass a few times. "Does this new man of yours have a name?"

Lauren nodded. "He does. His name is Keith."

"A promising start. Go on."

"Well," Lauren said, her face breaking out into a smile, "he's older than I originally thought he was. When I first met him, in a bookstore in Hamilton, I put his age at twenty-eight. But, it turned out he was almost ten years older. He doesn't own a motorcycle. In fact, at the time I met him, he didn't own much of anything."

At this point, Lauren paused in response to the smile that had broke onto Henri's face. "You're quite pleased with yourself, aren't you?"

Henri's smiled broadened. "I must admit, I'm quite enjoying myself, yes," he replied. "But, I'm sorry. I've interrupted. Please, go on. You were saying he didn't own much of anything. Not even a motorcycle. A bicycle, perhaps?"

Lauren shook her head. "No. Not even."

"Was he employed?"

"Part-time."

"Apartment or house?"

"Neither."

Henri raised his eyebrows. "Rooming house?"

"Oh no. Nothing like that. He had his own place. It was, um, it was more of a cottage, of sorts. I guess."

"A cottage?"

"Of sorts."

Henri gave Lauren a puzzled look. Then, winking at her, said, "Tell me, why do you like him so much?"

"Does it show?"

"Very much."

Lauren smiled. "I suppose I like him so much because he's the most fascinating person I've ever met."

"Well, now. That's quite the compliment. Do I get to know what so fascinates you?"

Lauren took a moment to consider the question. "Hmmm. Let's see. Aside from what you already guessed, about him being well-read and articulate and intelligent, what really made me think he was fascinating was when I found out where he lived. It was on our sixth date. We were walking back to my place again and I told him I thought it was odd I hadn't yet seen his place. He said it wasn't exactly the type of dwelling most women would like. I convinced him to let me be the judge of that and we turned around and started heading towards this forested area in Hamilton called Cootes Paradise. A few minutes later, after we'd walked down a long path, through some bushes, across a stream, and halfway up a hillside, he quickly opened a door in the side of the hill and we stepped into his place."

Henri stopped taking a sip of his scotch. "You mean . . . wait. What do you mean?"

"He lived in a large burrow in the side of a hill."

"I thought you said he lived in a cottage?"

"Of sorts." Lauren replied, smiling.

"You mean to tell me this was his . . . *residence*?"

Lauren nodded. "He built it himself."

Henri set his scotch glass down on the end table and clapped his hands together several times. "Bravo, my dear. Bravo. At long last, a love story worth hearing."

Lauren smiled, pleased by Henri's reaction. "I told you he was different."

"And now tell me, what did you think when you saw this burrow of his?"

"I thought it was the coolest place I'd ever been in."

"And did you spend much time there?"

"Quite a lot, in fact. It was actually very cozy."

"Good for you. And who or what, may I ask, inspired the construction of this unique residence?"

Lauren smiled. "A book."

"A book? Good heavens, which one?"

"*Walden*, by Henry David Thoreau. Keith's read it a dozen times."

"Well, now. I'm beginning to like this man of yours more by the minute. Good taste in women *and* literature."

"That's not all."

"You mean there's more?"

Lauren smiled. "After we'd spent a few more nights at his place, Keith showed me something. It was a lottery ticket he'd been holding onto for almost a year. It was the winning ticket. Two hundred and fifty thousand dollars."

"Two hundred and fifty thousand dollars?!"

Lauren nodded. "When we first met in the bookstore he had less than two months to cash it in or else it would be void."

Swiftly scooping up his scotch glass, Henri took another sip. "Two hundred and fifty thousand dollars. And he still chose to live in a cave?"

Lauren nodded. "For the rest of the summer and most of the fall."

"*Incroyable*," Henri said. "I take it this is no longer his principal residence, though?"

"No. He bought a nice little house in Hamilton's west end."

"And what about this other place?"

217

"Well, it just so happens there's a neat little story that goes along with this, too."

Henri smiled. "I was hoping so. Please, do tell. I'm all ears."

During the next five minutes or so, Henri listened as Lauren related the story of Keith discovering that his "secret" residence wasn't nearly as secret as he originally thought. In fact, it turned out he was actually being studied by a couple of fledgling anthropologists: an elderly man, Norman, and his granddaughter, Katie. Keith had seen the two of them hiking in and around Cootes Paradise before and had even spoken with Norman on one occasion. By early August, though, he became increasingly suspicious of them after seeing them several times in a short span and noticing things in the burrow had been moved around when he and Lauren weren't there. A few days later, after he and Lauren saw Norman and Katie approaching Cootes Paradise, Keith sent Lauren ahead to the burrow with instructions for her to exit it in half an hour. Initially, as he followed Katie and Norman at a safe distance, unable to eavesdrop on their conversation, Keith thought that perhaps he'd made a mistake, that perhaps Katie and Norman were merely avid birdwatchers. That was until he saw them settling into a hiding position behind a fallen log and taking turns training their binoculars at the spot on the side of the hill where the burrow was located. And then, when Lauren, at the pre-arranged time, exited the burrow, and the two of them went into a tizzy, Keith knew his secret was out. Close enough to easily hear them, Keith used the slight commotion caused by Lauren's exit to move to almost within reach of Norman and Katie before asking if he could borrow their binoculars to have a look at what had inspired all the excitement. Fortunately, both Katie and Norman were honest and embarrassed enough to admit what they'd been doing, and even permitted Keith to read the detailed notes Katie had made on him. And Lauren. A description of her appeared under the heading, "Preferred Mates & Mating Habits." Fortunately, she was the only entry in this particular chapter. In the end, Norman and Katie agreed to stop studying Keith and, later on in the fall, with Norman's permission, Keith gave the residence to Katie on two conditions: that she never tell anyone else about it, and that he and Lauren still be allowed to use it on occasion.

"Remarkable story, Lauren," Henri said, rising off the couch and making his way to the bar. "Quite the man you've got there."

"Thank you."

"Top up your glass for you?"

"Um, I'm okay, thank you."

After dropping a couple of fresh ice cubes into his whiskey tumbler and chasing it with a few ounces of Glenfiddich, Henri turned to Lauren. "Other than my grandson not being your type, how well do you know him?"

"Fairly well, I think."

"If I asked you a serious question, would you be honest with me?"

Lauren smiled. "I'll do my best."

"That's all I ask," Henri said, walking slowly back to the sectional sofa, this time taking a seat closer to Lauren. After studying her face for a few moments, he leaned towards her slightly. "Has my grandson told you which objects I am willing to him?" Henri asked, smiling as he watched Lauren's gaze travel immediately to the Persian rug.

Lauren nodded. "Yes, he told me."

"And what is he intending to do with them?"

"I believe he said he was interested in keeping the cigars."

"As I expected. He's been to an antiques dealer, hasn't he?"

"How did you know?"

"I saw him photographing the other pieces."

"He has some debts."

"Debts? Of what kind?"

"School loans. He's thinking of selling his car, actually."

"Really? I was under the impression he adores that car. I thought it was the reason he rarely drove it."

Lauren shook her head. "He said he can't afford to drive it."

"Hmmm," Henri said, sipping his scotch thoughtfully. "Interesting. Very interesting. I did not know this."

"I suppose you wouldn't if your relationship was solely confined to matters of business."

"*Touché*, Lauren," Henri said, smiling.

"May I ask you a question, Henri?"

"Of course."

"Was your *accident*, the one in the guest bathroom, planned?"

"Of course."

"Why would you do that?"

Henri shrugged. "The second guest bathroom hasn't seen a guest in more than five years."

"I meant why would you do *that?*"

"Oh, heavens. *That* wasn't me. I placed an order with one of the local transients the night before last."

"You mean you . . ." Lauren started to say, then, looking at Henri, she paused for a moment. "You mean you had someone else do it for you?"

Henri nodded. "He was kind enough to collect the raw materials and deliver the parcel to my front door by 11:00 AM this morning. It cost me twenty dollars. Plus another ten for shipping and handling."

"You're an absolute scoundrel."

"Thank you. If it's any consolation, I give Dennis's cousin, Maggie, an equally hard go of it."

"Shared misery is half misery?"

Henri chuckled. "In a manner of speaking, yes."

"You're not the least bit senile, are you?"

"Why? Is that the rumour?"

"The possibility came up."

Henry smiled. "And what is your conclusion?"

"I'm going to reserve judgement until after dinner."

"Smart woman. By the way, has Dennis told you why he comes here?"

Lauren nodded. "To cut the lawn, trim the hedges, clean the eave-stroughs, plant flowers, vacuum, work in the woodshop, run errands. And, on Saturdays, he stops by to drop off a novel for you."

Chuckling and nodding appreciatively, as though he'd just remembered a good joke he wanted to share, Henri tilted his head reflectively. "Well, now. That's interesting," he said.

"And why is that?"

"I thought for sure he would have told you the truth."

"That's not the truth?"

"Partly."

"What's the other part?"

"That, occasionally, one must stoop *and* scoop to conquer."

"Meaning?"

"You know, I believe I have forgotten my manners. Would you care for a tour of the house?"

"Is this your way of distracting me from the other part?"

"*Au contraire, mon amie.* So, a tour then?"

"Why not."

During the next twenty minutes, Henri led Lauren from room to room, bedroom to bathroom, kitchen to guest room, dining room to servants' quarters, allowing her to form her own opinion of each room without a steady narrative stream guiding her impression.

"It's beautiful, Henri," Lauren concluded, after they'd returned to the living room. "Very postmodern. Very . . . minimalist."

"You're holding something back, my dear."

Lauren shook her head.

"Go on, say it," Henri coaxed.

"From the outside, I was imagining the inside would look completely different from the way you have it and, well . . ."

"Yes?"

"Well, to be honest, it's not the style I think suits you."

"I couldn't agree more," Henri said. "Follow me. I want to show you something."

"Another accident?"

Henri smiled and led her to his den, the only room in the entire house he had yet to show her. Dressed completely in the darker wood tones of mahogany and oak, the den was the epitome of tradition, substance, and strength, immediately conjuring images of Bulls and Bears, scotch and cigars, bullion and business.

"Now, *this* is you," Lauren said. "Definitely you."

Henri smiled. "I must admit, this is my sanctuary."

"Did you have it professionally done?"

Henri pulled an album off the shelf behind his desk. "Have a look."

Lauren opened the album and began turning the pages. "Is this . . . Oh, my. This is your place, isn't it?"

Henri nodded, his eyes studying Lauren's expression as she continued turning the pages, admiring various other rooms decorated in the same style as the den.

"This is amazing."

"Better or worse?"

"Neither. It's just different."

Henri handed her another album. Then another. Then another. Each album was dated and had an overall theme — Asian minimalist, rustic farm-house, Spanish-French fusion, Art Deco — complete with subtle, secondary themes to complement or contrast the dominant decor.

"Are these real?" Lauren asked, fanning through the albums.

Henri nodded. "Very much so."

"So, someone didn't just render these using a computer graphics program or something?"

Henri shook his head. "No."

"You mean your house actually looked like this last year?" Lauren asked, pointing to the Spanish-French fusion theme.

"Yes."

Lauren glanced at Henri. "Why are you doing this?"

Henri shrugged. "I suppose I've always wanted to be a teacher."

"A teacher?"

Henri nodded. "When I was considerably younger, not much older than you are now, in fact, I harboured these delusions of becoming a great teacher. I think I had just read *The Symposium* or some other work outlining the teachings of Socrates, and fancied that I too, one day, might be responsible for instructing the youth of today. Have you read up on Socrates?"

Lauren shook her head.

"Pity. Not many your age do anymore. Anyway, having neither the academic standing nor the necessary mindset required to become a regular schoolteacher, I saw the only way around this obstacle was to open my own school. But what kind of school would it be? I asked myself. Who would attend? And, more importantly, who would pay to listen to me? That's right, my dear. It wasn't going to be one of these 'pay-what-you-can' or 'non-profit' institutions. I wasn't nearly as altruistic as I am now. Of course, I wasn't asking for much, not in comparison to what the likes of Montessori or Branksome or Upper Canada College charge. It would be just enough to pay the mortgage or rent of whatever home or building we were using, with some left over for supplies. Unfortunately, it wasn't until a few years ago I finally started up my school. And enrolled my first student."

Lauren regarded Henri for a moment. "You have a school?"

Henri nodded.

"Where?"

"You're standing in it."

"And your student?"

"Students. I have two students, now. Dennis and Maggie."

"You mean Dennis and Maggie have done all this?" Lauren asked, pointing at the albums.

Henri shook his head. "Just Dennis."

Lauren waited for the "*Je plaisant, mon amie*" comment but it didn't come. "You mean, he's done this all by himself?"

Henri nodded. "He's completely renovated my home five times in five years."

"That's . . . oh my God. That's amazing."

"Did you happen to notice the chaise lounge?" Henri said, gesturing to a dark wooden lounge chair facing the window, offering a view of the backyard garden and greenhouse.

Lauren nodded. "It's absolutely gorgeous."

"Dennis made that two years ago. Hand-carved it out of one piece of walnut."

"You're joking."

"I'm not. He's made several more pieces as well. The day bed in the first guest room. The rocking chair in the recreation room. The hutch in the dining room. The bar stools. Oh, and the Ukrainian-style deacon's bench you were admiring earlier in the front foyer."

"I can't believe this," Lauren remarked, shaking her head in amazement. "So, I guess you weren't lying when you said there was a reason for your horribleness."

Henri smiled. "And my horribleness does not end there. A man of my age and means doesn't come without some influence. I have almost a dozen friends who in some capacity or another are in the home design and architecture business. I've had a professional photographer come in and photograph and videotape the before, during, and after images of Dennis's work. It will be featured as part of a home design exhibit in the British, French, North American, and Australian editions of one of the leading design magazines. I have interviews lined up with TV, radio, and newspapers. In a few short weeks, Dennis will have enough work to keep him busy for the next two lifetimes."

"You're serious, aren't you?"

Henri nodded. "Without my dear grandson realising it, he has been an interior design apprentice for five years now."

"And he doesn't have a clue?"

Henri shook his head. "Not to my knowledge."

"When were you planning to tell him?"

"Tonight, actually. But then he brought you along and I became much too distracted."

Lauren smiled, a slight rouge colouring her cheeks, just as the phone rang.

"Excuse me," Henri said, walking towards the phone on the desk. "It's probably Dennis wanting to know if we want ketchup with our meal."

Lauren giggled.

Henri picked up the receiver. "Hello?"

. . . . To Be Continued . . .

can you tell us?

"Hello, Grandpa, how are you? . . . That's good. I'm looking forward to seeing you tomorrow . . . Yeah, I'll bring it . . . I won't forget . . . Six? I thought you said you were only having two guests? . . . So it's dinner for six now? I hope I have enough . . . Because I only bought ingredients for three . . . St. Lawrence and Kensington . . . Of course. I only buy fresh and I only buy things we can't get from the garden and greenhouse . . . I should. I'll just add another course or two of something else. Do any of the new guests have food allergies . . . No? Are you sure? . . . Okay, I'll see you tomorrow around three, then. Bye, Grandpa."

Maggie hung up the phone. "Bastard!" she said, wanting to spit on the sidewalk beside her.

Maggie had been her grandfather's personal cook for almost four years now. Three days a week she prepared meals for him and occasionally one or two of his guests. The fact that he'd suddenly changed it to "dinner for six" was typical of him. There had been dozens of times when she'd arrived at his home to find the number of guests had changed, usually from one to three or two to four or sometimes from four to none. And usually at least one of them was allergic to what she'd spent the previous day shopping for and/or preparing to cook. She hoped her grandfather wasn't lying to her about the additional guests and their non-existent food allergies.

Although she loved cooking, she despised the after-meal discussions with her grandfather and his guests. Traditionally, a collection of old farts who thought the idea of a good conversation was to compare her culinary skills to the various chefs they personally knew from their travels around the globe. Maggie had especially come to despise Vincent Voorallen. A Dutchman who had immigrated to Canada after running an extremely successful restaurant in Pennsylvania called Vincent the Vagabond, he was her grandfather's favourite chef. Her grandfather was constantly comparing the quality and presentation of her meals to Vincent's, which Maggie deemed remarkably unfair, seeing as Vincent had been a world-renowned chef who undoubtedly had dozens of minions and sous-chefs working for him during his heyday, while Maggie just had herself.

In addition to her culinary services, she was also the resident horti-culturist-in-training, spending a significant amount of her time tending to her grandfather's vegetable garden, fruit trees, and green-house. Though she often admitted to learning a lot from her grandfather, she always tempered her compliments with the fact that she considered him to be a monumental pain in the ass.

Leaning back in her patio chair, Maggie sighed, allowing herself to be transported from thoughts of her grandfather by the odyssey of sights (the Citytv building, the constant crush of cars and pedestrians, the starry evening sky); smells (cologne, coffee, cinnamon, and curry), and sounds (car horns, snatches of conversations, the "thwack-thwack-thwack" of a pair of stiff-soled shoes smacking the sidewalk) surrounding her.

Moments later, intrigued by the bit of dialogue she'd overheard as two women passed by her, Maggie tried to tune into their conversa-tion when they were forced to stop and wait for the light at the nearby intersection. After adjusting her auditory antennae, Maggie was able to block out just enough of the other noises to listen in.

"I can't believe Claudia's still with Phillip. That's . . . it's just not right."

"Hey, they still haven't found the weapons of mass destruction."

"That has to be the stupidest deal I've ever heard of."

"Hey, at least she's a woman of her word."

"Who cares? This is ridiculous. Something has to be done. We've got to rescue her."

"Maybe she doesn't want to be rescued. Maybe she's just one of these women who . . ."

The light had changed and the two women had now moved out of range, their conversation consumed by the static of competing street noises perforating the air along Queen West. A few moments later, the two young men taking a seat at the table next to Maggie filled the verbal void.

"You know what I wonder every time I'm in a place like this?" the young man wearing the white dress shirt and casual dress slacks said.

"What, you mean a coffee shop?"

"It doesn't have to be a coffee shop, just a franchise store — like Second Cup or McDonalds or Starbucks or even the Gap. Every time I'm in a place like this, I can't help wondering if there's someone just like me sitting in the same place in some other city. Like, someone who is wearing basically what I'm wearing, drinking what I'm drinking, kind of like a cookie cutter version of me, you know? It'd be so cool to find out what he was thinking and —"

"Why don't you find out?"

"Excuse me?" the guy wearing the white dress shirt said, turning and frowning at Maggie.

"Why don't you find out?" Maggie replied, leaning forward in her chair, smiling.

"What are you talking about?"

"Pick a city," Maggie said, reaching for her cell phone.

The two young men exchanged glances. A moment later, the guy wearing the white dress shirt shrugged. "Um, okay. How about Oakville? No, wait. Make it Hamilton. I know there's a Second Cup in Westdale Village."

"Okay, Hamilton it is. And where is it, again? In Westdale?"

"Yep."

"One moment. I'm just calling directory assistance . . . Hamilton . . . No . . . Second Cup in Westdale."

A few moments later, Maggie dialled the number.

"Yeah, hi. Are you busy? . . . Can you spare a few moments? . . .

Great. Okay, this may seem odd but I'm looking for someone. He's left me all these clues of where he's going to be and I'm supposed to try and figure it out . . . Yeah, exactly. It's exactly like that *Where's Waldo?* . . . Um, let's see. He's about six feet tall. Average build. Clean cut. Sort of looks like a cross between Matt Damon with darker hair and fewer moles and a mannequin in a Gap store window. He's probably wearing a dress shirt, possibly a white one, with beige khakis and he'll be drinking a cappuccino. Anyone there matching that description? . . . There is? No way, really? . . . That's awesome! Can you put him on the line? . . . Um, I don't know, maybe just tell him it's an old friend from school. No, I know, ask him his name and when he tells you, say, 'She's got you!' and then tell him the phone is for him. Oh, oh, and when you do, can you get back to the phone first and tell me his name? . . . Thanks, you're amazing. *Vive la* Second Cup!" Maggie shouted, before covering her cell phone and telling the two guys, "She's going to get him."

"This is insane," the guy with the white dress shirt said. "You're insane."

"Hey, you wanted to know. Yeah, hi . . . Cody? That's him, thanks," Maggie said, smiling. "Here he — oh, hi. Cody? . . . Yeah, hi. I was just wondering what you were thinking roughly a minute or two before the clerk came over and got you . . . Maggie . . . Toronto . . . No, it's not a joke. See, there's this guy sitting beside me and he's always wondered if there was someone who looked like him, sitting in the same franchised store as he was only in some other city and, apparently, you fit the bill . . . All he wants to know is what you were thinking? Can you tell us?"

. . . . To Be Continued . . .

he's pretty persuasive . . . .

"Actually, I'm kinda busy . . . I'm on a date . . . It's going fairly well, thank you . . . Listen, lady, I don't know what to tell you . . . I guess I was thinking that if I end up marrying this woman I'd have a pretty cool story to tell my kids . . . Because I got in an accident because of her . . . Today . . . I rear-ended some guy . . . Yeah. And then I went over and asked her out . . . Thanks. Anyway, I should probably get back to her . . . It was nice talking to you, too. Bye."

Cody handed the phone back to the clerk and returned to his seat on the patio outside Second Cup. "Sorry about that," he said to Jenna, once again feeling a pang of pleasure at the sight of her body wrapped tightly in her black lycra halter dress. He was glad she hadn't changed her outfit since their meeting on Locke Street a few hours ago.

"No problem," Jenna replied, smiling. "Something important?"

"No, not at all. In fact, I think that might be the most bizarre phone call I've ever received."

"Care to share?"

"You probably won't believe me if I tell you. Besides, I'm more interested in what we were talking about. You were saying you're an actress?"

"No, not really. I'm just doing a workshop of sorts, getting experience. That sort of thing."

"By pretending to be a hooker?"

"Among other things."

"Isn't that a little dangerous?"

"It can be. But it's worth it. Besides, it's just acting. You get to take it as far as you want."

"And you said your father gave you the idea for this?"

Jenna nodded. "He does the same thing."

"Your father goes around pretending he's a hooker?"

"No, silly. He's goes around pretending he's someone else. He came across this book a while back about this group of faux friends from Toronto who go around pretending to be people they're not, duping everyone, even their close friends and relatives because they're part of this avant-garde acting school."

"So, what, he's doing the same thing?"

Jenna nodded. "My father's played some pretty neat characters."

"Such as?"

"Um, he's played an Italian mafia guy, a high-rolling CEO, a down-and-out bum, a garbage collector . . . tons of different people."

"Does he have a favourite character?"

Jenna smiled, coyly. "Jacques the Frenchman."

"Jacques the Frenchman, huh? And what exactly does Jacques the Frenchman do?"

"His specialty is wining and dining vulnerable women."

"I take it your parents are divorced."

Jenna nodded. "Of course. And it's not as bad as I make it sound. He doesn't go around taking advantage of these women. It's more of an equitable exchange."

"How so?"

"Well, if the woman is having marital problems, for instance, my father might persuade her to have a passionate affair with him."

"And how is that an equitable exchange?"

Jenna shrugged. "He gets to play out a role and the woman gets to have an affair to remember."

"Is he always able to persuade them?"

Jenna nodded. "I've seen him in action. He's pretty persuasive. Of course, it doesn't hurt when the setting for his seduction is Montreal."

"Is that where he does it?"

"Of course," Jenna said, smiling. "Where else but in the Paris of North America?"

Cody took a reflective sip of cappuccino. "So, how does your father do it?"

"What do you mean?"

"I mean, how does he pick the person he's going to seduce? How does he know she's vulnerable? How does he seduce her?"

Jenna smiled. "Well, first of all, practice makes perfect. And my father's had lots of practice in the past few years since he read that book. The first thing he does is select a location that attracts a certain type of tourist. Like this place, for instance. Places like Second Cup or Starbucks are ideal. And that's because people, and especially tourists travelling alone who don't speak the language very well, inevitably seek out the familiar. They see a McDonalds or a Starbucks and they think, 'Whew, I know this place. It's got the same set-up as the ones they have in my country or city.' So, my father will usually camp out in a place like this and wait until the right woman comes along. Once he finds her — usually an anglophone woman in her mid-thirties to early fifties who he knows is by herself and is a first-time visitor to Montreal — he'll make up some excuse to talk to her. Then, after they've been chatting for a while, he'll drop into this whole routine of his about him being the owner of a bistro and how demanding the work is. He speaks fluent French, and in his suave French accent, he'll tell her how all he used to do was work, work, work, that his bistro occupied all his time until, finally, one day he realised working this much wasn't healthy and he needed to take a break and go on vacation. The next thing you know they're strolling through Old Montreal, having dinner on some *café-terrasse* overlooking the St. Lawrence River and the woman is putty in his hands."

Cody smiled and shook his head. "Wow. I can't imagine pulling off something like that."

Lauren shrugged. "All it takes is some practice."

"Yeah, and a whole lot of balls."

"That's my father."

Cody laughed. "So, exactly how many ladies has Jacques from Montreal seduced?"

"He's not from Montreal."

"I thought you said he —"

"He seduces them in Montreal. But he tells them he's from New Orleans."

"New Orleans? Wait a second, your father is *Jacques from New Orleans?*"

"Yeah. Why?"

"He wouldn't happen to be in Montreal right now, would he?"

Jenna nodded. "He left yesterday, actually."

"Is he doing this acting thing of his there?"

Jenna shrugged. "I don't know. Probably."

"Holy shit," Cody said, abruptly standing up and reaching into his front pant pocket for his cell phone.

"What's wrong?"

"Um, ah . . . nothing," Cody replied, now frantically searching the call directory on his cell phone for his mother's number. "Where did you say you and your father are from, again?"

. . . . **To Be Continued . . .**

The stories continue in Volume Three
Spring 2007 . . .

SHANNON LEENDERS

Gordon j.h. Leenders is the author of *May Not Appear Exactly As Shown* and *To Be Continued . . . volume one.*

Thanks to:
Jack David, for number three. Jen Hale, for your suggestions, support, and another quick and easy edit. Nadine James, for your encouragement, understanding, and ongoing promotional efforts. Kulsum, Joy, Tania, David, Mary, and the rest of the ECW gang, for your assistance. Montreal, Hamilton, Niagara Falls, and Toronto for your inspiration. My father, Henry, for laying the foundation. My wife, Shannon, for always being there. My son, Mason, for the immeasurable joy you've brought into my life.

— Gordon j.h. Leenders
tobecontinued123@hotmail.com